Graphics Design: Tom Rye

Special thanks to Ed, Robyn, and Sophie.

Glossary

Aurum - The proper name for the Golden Realm. A dimension that is home to keepers and The Creator's armies.

Cast - A colorful, mist-like energy that some nephilim are able to form into weapons.

Challavenge - The region to the northeast of Hazdrim's mainland. Primarily consists of mountains and evergreen forests. Challavenge has no official capital because their nilaon and three highrindh live nomadic lifestyles between their villages and towns.

Drundra - The region to the north of Hazdrim's mainland. Primarily consists of rivers, plains, and swamps. Drundra is the most scientifically and technologically advanced of the five regions. It's primary source of trade is wine and food-stuffs. Drundra has an alliance with Venner and is in its second great war with Challavenge. Its capital is The Villa.

Foald - The primary currency in Hazdrim.

Golovarn - The region to the southeast in Hazdrim's mainland. Primarily consists of jungles with prairies to the south. Despite being the largest region, Golovarn has the lowest population. This region is known for its dangerous flora and fauna. It's primary sources of trade are rubber and lumber. Golovarn has an official alliance with Venner. Their capital is The Bastion.

Hazdrim - The proper name for the Nephilim Realm. A dimension between earth and the Golden Realm. The nephilim afterlife.

Hex - A female magus.

Highrindh - One of the three "generals" of a region.

Keeper - A species of deity commonly confused with angels, demons, habes, and gods. Keepers serve The Creator. Unlike angels, keepers have free-will and a soul.

Mage - A male magus.

Magus - A species with the ability to manipulate sensory perception by using spells.

Nephilim - A human with keeper genetics.

Nephilim-Magus - A cross between a Nephilim and a Magus. They carry the traits of both species.

Nilaon - The leader of a Hazdrim region.

Notam - A complex branding cast that binds two individuals, the brander and the branded. The brander has the ability to use the brand to track the branded. This cast is almost exclusively used by Nilaon on their Highrindh.

Regions - The five political areas of Hazdrim.

Spell - Incantations used by magus and nephilim-magus. There are five commonly known magus spells, each used to manipulate the senses.

Tavdren - The region to the northwest in Hazdrim's mainland. Primarily consists of forests and mountains. Tavdren is a military oriented region with the largest army. It's main sources of trade are steel, leather, and fish. Tavdren has no official alliances but has friendly relationships with Venner and Challavenge. Their capital is The Fort.

The Physicians - A cult-like group which operates the Waking Center and determines when nephilim awaken in Hazdrim. They have numerous labs in Venner.

The Waking - The event of nephilim waking up in the afterlife that takes place in the Waking Center. Historically, the waking occurred annually, however, the physicians change the date to once every decade.

Venner - The region to the southwest in Hazdrim's mainland. Primarily consists of plains, islands, and small canyons. Venner has good relations with neighboring regions because it has not instigated wars and has no border conflicts. They are a trading center for a variety of products including wool, fish, and glass. Venner is the only region that is not led by a nilaon. Instead, they are governed by a council. The mainland is not protected by an army, but powerful Vennarian Knights. The capital is the Citadel.

Wakers - A term used to describe newly awakened nephilim.

.....

"The Nephilim were on the earth in those days-and also afterward-when the sons of God went to the daughters of humans and had children by them. They were the heroes of old, men of renown."
-Genesis 6:4, NIV

.....

If he was ever going to survive there, he would need to control the web.

.....

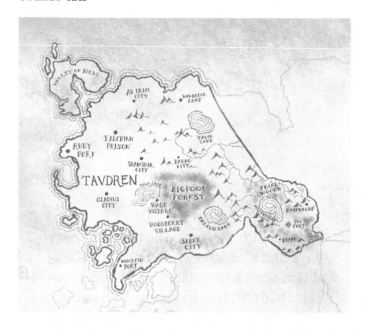

Hazdrim (Nephilim Realm)

Prologue

The morning sun beat upon the ground at Lawan's feet. She blinked her sharp, maroon eyes, not diverting her attention from the barn. She was waiting.

If she was anything, she was patient.

Lawan had a pale, ethereal face with high cheekbones and a dangerous slant to her full lips. White hair flowed past her shoulders. A minuscule white scar adorned her right cheek. Hers was a harsh beauty.

She wore a velvet cloak that fell the length of her statuesque frame. Her leather boots made no indentation on the dirt beneath her. She was a shadow.

Lawan knew her curse. It was cruel, merciless, and perfect. She didn't care about the centuries of personal suffering. All that mattered to this deity was that her enemies also suffer.

A tall boy emerged from the barn. He

walked past Lawan without seeing her. To him life was simple. Youth spared him the challenges of adulthood. The boy couldn't comprehend the threat Lawan posed.

She could sense that he was a magus with strong casting ability. Other skills would reveal themselves later, but for now, his casting was enough to satisfy Lawan.

There is no alternative.

As she watched, the boy stumbled over a rock, nearly tipping the pail of milk he carried. Lawan realized her hopes for revenge could be accomplished.

She'd first visited her son, the boy's father, but he'd been strong-willed. She would've had difficulty breaking him.

He died before she'd made her final decision.

The boy is all I have.

Her grandson was her only hope. He was Lawan's last chance for revenge.

.....

Part One

.....

O'MERIT KAY

Chapter One

In southeastern Georgia, on the outskirts of Savannah, was a modest sweet potato farm that belonged to the McClanon family. It was small but well managed and thus profitable.

There were crop fields on the north and south of the property with one long out-building off to the side for the work hands. Next to this was an unpainted barn stocked with hens, several roosters, a donkey, a handful of hogs, and two milk cows, Dolly and Marmalade. The stables housed three workhorses and a slew of lazy barn cats. This farm had been in the McClanon family for generations.

Situated central to this was the large McClanon farmhouse, freshly painted white every decade per Mrs. McClanon's instructions.

There was a wide porch that wrapped around the house. It provided plenty of shade for the rockers and two dogs, Bird and Brick. The house was two stories with a basement cellar. Behind was the smokehouse, and not far beyond that was the small peach orchard started by great grandfather, Billford McClanon.

They were a proud family with no secrets or scandals and were respected in the community and generally liked by their neighbors. Through the generations, good and some bad, the McClanon family had a far-reaching effect on the area. Especially the current Mrs. McClanon who avidly participated in the social life of the nearby town of Waller.

The patriarch of the family, Jacob McClanon, was an honorable man. Despite the economic pressures of his occupation, Mr. McClanon refused to own slaves. It was a peculiar stance that raised eyebrows, but not enough to cast a shadow over his name.

Although he'd avoided being scarred by gossip throughout his life, there was one thing Mr. McClanon couldn't avoid. Not long after Jacob was blessed with the news of his third child being conceived, tragedy struck. The country split and went to war with itself. Mr. McClanon was drafted into the confederate army and was never to set foot on the farm again.

He never met his third child.

Jacob McClanon died in a medic tent a

hundred miles from his home at the age of thirty-four.

His brother, Daniel McClanon, wasn't drafted due to a childhood injury to his right leg. He slid into the role of patriarch as news of Jacob's death reached the family. In the interim he'd overseen the farm and had little time to grieve his brother's passing. The farm was bringing in the harvest. Despite being unable to do much physical work on the farm, he kept it running.

The lady of the house was Gwen McClanon. She was a tall woman with lovely but stern features. Although she was admired, she was also easily cross. She'd been happily married to Jacob for fourteen years, yet Gwen easily settled into being a flawless widow. The death of her husband struck her hard, but she would never let grief mar her presentation. She turned out very well in widow black and wore it for the remainder of her days.

Widow McClanon and Jacob had three biological daughters and one eldest adopted son. The twin daughters were Elizabeth and Ellen. They were very bright with a keen interest in stirring up mischief. Ellen was the worse of the two.

The youngest daughter, Maggie, was named after the Widow's sister, Margaret. She was a happy child who spent her days in the nursery. Elizabeth took a special interest in her younger sister and was a great help to the Widow.

Their adopted son was Douglas. He was so beloved by Daniel McClanon that he was promised to inherit the farm. Because of Daniel's injury, Douglas did most of the work on the farm, assisted by three hired hands.

Douglas stood apart from his adopted family. While they were fair, except for Ellen whose rough nature brought her sunshine and bruises, he was dark-complexioned. His appearance was made all the more unusual by his bright silver-streaked hair and storm gray eyes. He had poor eyesight, which required a pair of thick oval spectacles.

He was fifteen years old, but with his large frame, he could easily pass for a grown man. Standing at six feet and eight inches, he was considered a giant in the area.

He had a rolling soft Savannah accent, unlike his adopted family, who took their tone from the Widow. Her people came from Smyrna outside Atlanta and had a distinctly different lilt in their voices, of which she encouraged and was proud.

Douglas was closer to Ellen than Elizabeth because she was spoiled and cared only for schoolwork and the baby. Ellen enjoyed spending time outdoors with him and sneaking off into the fields whenever she could. They spent long hours together with Sampson, fishing the back pond in contented silence.

The farm absorbed the death of Jacob. Harvest didn't stop. Douglas bore the hardest burden of his adopted father leaving for war. He'd been pulled from school to assist his uncle. The news of Jacob's death meant Douglas would never return to his studies. To the family, the primary fear was Douglas being drafted upon his sixteenth birthday. Rumors had been spreading that groups were in the area collecting boys of an even younger age.

Nevertheless, Mrs. McClanon made sure the family ran just as smoothly as ever. The girls arrived at school on time, the chores were finished before midday, and they attended church every Sunday. The McClanon family would not fall easily.

·····

Douglas sat on a worn, wooden stool in the barnyard. He tossed a small leather ball up and down. It was a childhood gift from Mr. McClanon. A gift he would treasure for years to come.

His mind blocked out the sounds of the barn. The quarter horses snorted and stomped in their stalls, eager for sunshine and a nibble of fresh grass. A barn cat, Rumble, stalked after an unsuspecting cricket. The work dogs, Brick and Bird, were noisily scuttle-butting over a corn sack.

He'd finished the morning chores early

and had some time to himself to sit and watch the dust curl in a stream of sunlight. The new hay in the loft smelled sweet. The girls were off at school, and his friend Sampson was in the back milking the dairy cows. He had a few free minutes to sit in the shade of the barn, enjoying the peace.

His sharp eyes watched the ball fly in the air and land back into his rough hand. He tossed it up again, mouthing the word "up" to himself.

It fell back to him. "Down."

Toss. "Up."

Fall. "Down."

He did this for a while. It helped focus his mind.

The ball missed his fingers and rolled toward the stalls. A small mud crusted boot stopped the ball and gently kicked it to Douglas. The owner of the boot was a young, dark-skinned boy. His generous, warm smile and silky brown eyes lit up his face. Sampson was a hand on the farm.

The McClanons had bought him to prevent the boy from being sold to a North Carolina tobacco farm. Jacob had granted him his freedom that very day. Having nowhere else to go, Sampson lived in the bunkhouse with the two other hands and worked the farm as a free and hired man. In addition to his small pay, he received meals for his work on the farm.

"What happened to, 'I *have the quickest*

hands in Georgia?' Huh?" Sampson teased. His voice was thick with Georgia drawl. Douglas scooped up the ball and put it in his pocket.

"Ah shut it. Did Marmalade give ya any trouble with the milking?"

Sampson slumped down next to him. "Na. She's a real sweetheart."

"Ole girl usually gives me lots of trouble."

"She jus' likes me better."

Douglas could not resist chuckling along with his friend. He absentmindedly fiddled with the ball in his pocket. "How long till the girls get home?"

Sampson tilted his head and tried to get a view of the sun. "A few hours. I think."

"When do we start plowin'?"

"Well, if today is Friday...'bout three months I reckon." Sampson laughed at his jest.

Douglas slid off the stool. Having the harvest in and the cool fall months ahead would be dull. "What are we gonna do?"

Douglas began pacing the barn. His fingers closed around the ball as he resumed tossing it. It was his habit.

.....

Chapter Two

The two young girls strolled down the dirt road to the house. Elizabeth was deep into her book. She paid hardly any attention to her sister or the path ahead.

Ellen was skipping happily, making her pigtails dance. Her tin lunch pail swayed back and forth at her side. Unlike her sister, she was alert to everything they passed.

Douglas and Sampson were throwing rocks at the trees stirring birds into the air when they heard the girls coming. Sampson snapped his fingers to alert Douglas. Grabbing a handful of pebbles, the boys began tossing them at the girl's feet as they crested the hill.

Elizabeth squealed at the initial onslaught of pebbles and darted towards the house. She held the book defensively over her head, causing the boys to double over with laughter.

Ellen snarled and chucked one of the rocks back. It hit Sampson square in the forehead causing him to yelp and duck behind Douglas.

"Back off, Elliemean. We was only teasin'."

"Elliemean?"

"Yea. Fits, donnit?"

"Lick a slop bucket!" Ellen yelled, throwing another rock.

Using Douglas as a human shield, Sampson hollered, "She's gone mad!"

Ellen hooted a war cry and charged the boys swinging her pail. Douglas chuckled and stepped in her way. "Let him be."

Ellen and Sampson were eight years old. Douglas was a wall between the pair.

"Y'all started it!"

Sampson grabbed a stick and held it like a sword. "Come at me!" He shouted, peering around the large boy between them.

Ellen gladly accepted the challenge, and soon the two were running along the road playing pirate.

Douglas smiled and watched the pair. He cleaned his glasses and walked past the barn. Kicking a pinecone down the dirt path, he smiled as Bird yipped and gave chase. Brick beat her to it, and within seconds, the two mutts had forgotten all about the pinecone and were wrestling each other.

Douglas snickered and patted Bird's head when the two calmed down. Her tail wagged along with the pats, making loud thumps against his dusty trousers. A sudden bark from Brick made the pats and rubs come to a sudden stop.

Douglas sighed and turned. He assumed that Brick was jealous of Bird's attention, but to his surprise, the large mutt was growling towards the woods just past the barn. His bark was a warning, alerting the boy to a bobcat nearby.

Douglas nodded and narrowed his eyes at the tree line. After a couple of seconds, Bird had joined Brick in the hostile growling.

He was curious but knew from experience to be cautious. The boy cleaned his glasses hoping to get a better look. When he took them off, he noticed not a wildcat but a white blur standing upright next to the barn.

What is that?

Douglas slipped the glasses back on. The white shape was gone. He stared hard at the spot for another moment, thinking the shadows had been playing tricks on him.

Ignoring his gut, he whistled to the dogs and sped up his pace toward the house for supper. The dogs followed him to the porch where they would wait under the steps for their evening meal of table scraps.

.....

Chapter Three

Douglas took his place at the table next to Sampson and Elizabeth. He yawned and slouched in the chair. He didn't think anything of the white figure. And didn't want to.

It was custom for the hands to sit at the end of the table, furthest from the widow. They were always welcome to dine with the family provided they were clean and mannerly.

The family prayed and quietly ate. Widow McClanon chatted with Daniel about the war. Ever since Jacob's death, suppers were not the same. Worry over the war and the effect it had on the farm permeated most conversations.

Ellen tried to hide the dirt under her fingernails. She knew her mother wouldn't approve. Her green eyes slid sideways over to Sampson, who couldn't resist the urge to laugh. She kicked his foot under the table.

Douglas smirked and tried to avoid being caught up in the exchange, but when Sampson accidentally kicked him instead of Ellen, he was forced to join. The three were all shot down by a disapproving glance from Widow McClanon.

"Children."

"Sorry." The three said simultaneously.

Elizabeth rolled her eyes and placed her fork down. "Am I the only child here that has manners?"

"Elizabeth, the situation has been handled."

"Yes ma'am." She mumbled defeatedly. Ellen stuck her tongue out at her sister.

The family resumed their quiet conversation. Douglas stared out the window, where he had a wide view of the barn. The white blur popped back into his memory, and his mind ran over what all it could have been.

He was whisked back to reality when he heard Daniel calling him.

"Doug? Can you hear me?"

"Yes, sir. Sorry."

"Did ya turn the horses into da pasture?"

"Yes, sir."

Gwyn lifted an eyebrow and gave him *her stare*. "You seem distracted?"

"The dogs spooked meh. Dats all."

Her attention turned to the girls. "How

was school today?"

As talk dwindled, Douglas found himself staring out at the barn. Again, he allowed his mind to replay what he had seen, or imagined, from earlier. He must have lost track of time because before he knew it, dinner was over, and he was giving Brick and Bird the scraps.

Douglas placed the dish of leftovers on the porch. Brick and Bird bounded over and devoured the food. He stepped back and yawned. "Dat enough for ya?"

They responded with eager barking and tail wagging.

Unexpectedly, the barks turned to the low growling from earlier. Douglas felt the hairs on his arms spring. He could feel something out there as much as the dogs. He didn't investigate, but hurriedly turned his back and went inside.

.....

He barely slept that night. Usually, the ball calmed him before bed, but tonight was different. It was colder. He was uneasy in his body and his mind as superstitious thoughts wandered to the white shape.

Was it a ghost?

The chiming of the hallway clock kept his mind spinning.

Bong.

What if?

Bong.

Maybe?

He knew this was just foolish worry.

.....

Chapter Four

The next day was Saturday. As usual on McClanon farms, Ellen insisted on playing in the nearby swampy woods. She managed to drag Sampson and Doug along. With harvest in, their morning chores were quickly finished.

"Let's make a game!" She yapped like a puppy before clumsily leaping over a log.

Douglas shrugged, sharpening the tip of a walking stick with his pocketknife as he walked. "I'm kinda tired."

"What? Nah! It's Saturday! Dat means we play!"

Sampson snickered and bounced over the log after Ellen. "Yeah, Doug." He almost fell into a tree.

"Fine. I'm comin'." Douglas easily jumped

the log.

Ellen grabbed a stick and pointed it at the air. "Good! We have a lot ta do!"

Sampson shivered at her determined tone.

Douglas stifled a yawn.

They went farther into the swamp. It took all of Douglas' willpower to keep from falling asleep whenever he sat down. He itched to go back home and nap in the sunshine on a porch rocker.

"How long till we go?" He mumbled under his breath. Fortunately, Ellen did not hear. She would have smacked him if she had.

Sampson chuckled, catching his friend complaining. He picked up a pebble and aimed it at the back of Ellen's head. Before he had a chance to throw it, she stopped in front of him. "Let's build a fort!"

"A fort? Sure."

Douglas rolled his eyes. He rubbed his glasses clean against his untucked shirttail. When he put them back on, he noticed a strange shape slithering under a log on which Sampson was standing.

He adjusted his glasses to get a better look. "Da hell..." His eyes widened and he charged into Sampson, pushing him from off the log. "Water moccasin!"

"Ahh!" The smaller boy screamed.

The two watched in terror as the snake

opened its pearly white mouth and curled into a ball. Douglas remembered his father's instructions for dealing with the dangerous creature.

Kill it as quickly as you can. Bury the head in the ground.

If bitten with company, lay down and try not to move while they get help.

If bitten when alone, pray.

Sampson yelled and hid behind Ellen, who was hissing back at the snake.

Douglas jabbed the sharpened point of his walking stick at the snake's head with enough force to kill it instantly.

"Poke it again!" Ellen shouted encouragement, "Crush it!"

"Ahh!" Sampson shrieked.

"Will ya two jus' calm down?"

"Kill it!"

"Sampson, ya slaughtered hogs. Ellen, stop bein' hysterical."

"It almost killed meh!" Sampson kicked the snake's writhing tail.

"Beh careful. The fangs still carry poison. I'll have ta bury it," Douglas warned his young friend.

Ellen sighed and patted Douglas' back. "Good job kid. I would ya jus' smashed it under meh shoe."

Douglas ignored her comment and dug a shallow hole with his now bloodstained stick.

The three were interrupted by the faint

sound of horses. The visitors had to be coming up from the path that parted the woods. The three exchanged confused glances.

.....

Chapter Five

Douglas and Ellen hurried back to the house. Sampson went off to the bunkhouse.

"It sounded like a group," Ellen mumbled as she stepped from the tree cover.

"The war is comin' closer." Douglas nodded and walked past her and glanced over at the house. Stepping off the porch were a half dozen Confederate soldiers. His heart raced. The widow must have run them off because the men had been inside the house only a short time.

"Guess so." Ellen was more worried than him.

"I'm sure it won't go on much longer."

She softly replied, "That's what Daddy said before he left."

"How do you even remember dat? You were just a tot." Her brother didn't know how to comfort her, but the gentle teasing seemed to help. Ignoring the slaps on his arm, Douglas led her through the back door.

.....

Widow McClanon paced the parlor rug. Douglas fidgeted with his wooden ball next to Daniel, who sat in a high-backed chair by the window. He was smoking his pipe and wore a frown.

"I won't leave this farm to them. I don't care what the lieutenant said." Widow McClanon's proud voice filled the room.

"Unfortunately, Gwen, we may not have a choice if the fighting moves this way," Daniel flipped through the papers the lieutenant had left.

Widow McClanon smacked Douglas' hands. "We are in da middle of a crisis. Put dat ball down."

"Yes, ma'am." He slipped the ball back into his pocket. "Why am I here anywa'?" He instantly regretted using that tone for it was followed by another hand slap.

Widow McClanon resumed her agitated pacing. She moved with intention and thought. Her will was dominant over the entire house. "Y'all will have ta drag my mangled dead corpse off dis farm."

"Gwyn..." Daniel drawled, clenching the

pipe between his teeth.

"It is Mrs. McClanon." She smiled coolly at Daniel, coming to a sudden halt in her pacing. Her fists rested on her hips.

The three fell into a long, tense silence. It was finally broken by Daniel when he sighed, puffed the pipe between his lips, and quietly left the room with his newspaper. He patted the boy's back on his way.

"Her pride will ruin us." Douglas heard his uncle mumble.

Whether Widow McClanon heard it or not, she remained silent. She shut her eyes and sat in an armchair with her hands clasped in her lap.

Douglas fidgeted with the ball in his pocket and offered a weak smile. "We won't needa' leave da farm."

"Son..." She rubbed her forehead. "...there are bad people in dis world. Bad people that will rip innocent lives apar'."

"I know, mother."

"No, ya don't. And I hope you won't ever have ta." Her eyes were narrowed with a lioness' determination.

He forced himself to make eye contact. "You don't have ta worry 'bout me." Once again, he was filled with the fear of being drafted. Widow McClanon sensed this and returned his smile.

Growing up with Widow McClanon as a

mother was not easy. She was often cold and always strictly principled. However, she was fiercely loyal and very loving to the people she cared about.

"I won't leave."

"I know, Mother."

.....

Chapter Six

Douglas was in a deep sleep.

He stood at the top of a grassy hill, watching a building in flames. His vision was blurry, similar to when his glasses were removed.

"Watch it burn," A sharp voice sounded next to him. The voice was distinctly female, yet it was raspy and strained. Different from anything he had heard before.

He turned to whom the voice belonged. Beside him was the strange white blur. He tried to get a better look, but he was fixed in place. His actions were not his to control. His emotions were as blurred as the figure itself.

An unrecognizable voice came from inside him. "I don't boast." His own voice was different.

Older and harsh.

A realization began to form slower than the dawning sun. There was something his mind wanted to grab hold of, yet it remained elusive. And as quickly as it started, the dream was over.

.....

Several months had passed since the soldiers' visit. Early spring was upon them, and the farm had begun preparations for the next plowing.

When Douglas turned twenty, Daniel would officially pass on the farm to him. To prove himself capable of the responsibility, he doubled his chores. The next day would be Douglas' sixteenth birthday.

Douglas was checking the fence line that bordered their pastures. When finished, he took the lane toward home. His quarter horse, a small and sturdy bay with white socks, was named Sizzle. He was a workhorse.

Douglas led Sizzle around to the main road. Troops had been passing through Waller, so it was no surprise to him when he saw a small band on the road ahead. What shocked him was that they were knocking on the Brooks' door.

Tapping Sizzle's sides, he hurried across the road. The soldiers were collecting the Brooks boy. His heart fell into his gut. The Brooks boy was just over fifteen. Douglas knew that their farm was next.

They're desperate.

The war ain't going well for 'em.

He tightened the reins on Sizzle and steered him across the road. One of the soldiers call out in his direction. "Hey! Boy! Come here!"

Douglas panicked and squeezed Sizzle's sides with his knees, bringing the horse to a canter and then a full gallop. As he rode onto his property, he could hear the soldier still yelling to get his attention.

His glasses slid down his nose.

What if they come for me?
What if they take me away?

Sizzle's hooves thundered down the path to the barn. Douglas had been riding since he was a child, but the overwhelming fear of the soldiers clouded his senses. Before he could prevent it, Sizzle charged the barn, stopping hard just before crashing into the stable wall. Douglas lunged forward and into the horse's neck, grunting as the horse reared.

At the commotion, Sampson rushed out from the milking pen. "Da Hell?" He grabbed the reins and helped his friend off the horse. The boy led Sizzle into his stall where he quickly rubbed the horse down after the hard run.

Douglas slumped against the barn wall. "Ow-w, man."

Sampson called from within the stall. "What da hell did ya do?"

"They took da Brooks boy." Douglas explained, watching the boy brush Sizzle's sides.

"Did they see ya?" He asked, then his eyes widened with understanding.

"Yea-a."

Finished, Sampson extended his hand. Douglas took the hand and hoisted himself onto his feet. It took a few stumbles before he stood balanced.

The two boys walked back to the house silently. Neither wanted to talk about the inevitable. That the soldiers would know where to find him.

.....

Chapter Seven

Douglas couldn't sleep that night. His mind wouldn't give him peace over being drafted. He didn't want to spread fear to his family, so he'd kept the earlier events to himself.

Sampson had wanted to stay with him, but Douglas refused. That would only raise suspicion around the house and worry the girls.

Perched on the edge of his bed, he tossed the ball.

Up.

The house is deep off the track. Maybe they won't find me.

Down.

Of course, they will.

Up.

They'll come.

Down.

Henry Brooks. Small and bulky, with black hair and blue eyes, was notorious for his big mouth. He and Douglas had a contentious history. A few years ago, Henry and some of his boys had tried to mess with Sampson. Douglas stopped them before Sampson was hurt. There had been no punches thrown, but words were said that could never be forgiven.

It wouldn't be out of character for the Brooks boy to tell the soldiers about Douglas and where he lived. That thought added to Douglas' list of worries.

Out of the still, quiet night, there came a startling, holy hell from the dogs. The commotion could mean only one thing.
They're here.
Even in the night, I am not safe from the soldiers.

.....

Douglas hurried into his work clothes and shoved his ball into a pocket, and on silent feet, he slipped down the hall. Widow McClanon was mysteriously dressed and waiting at the large front door. In his mind, he knew there was something unusual about her being dressed and ready. She'd been expecting it.

Widow McClanon nodded briefly to her adopted son.

"Mom…"

"Sh." She shook her head and sighed, "No need. I sent everyone back to bed."

"Is it..."

"Yes." At the sound of boots on the front porch, she opened the front door and stared at the soldier who was approaching the doorway. "Ya better have a good reason for waking this house."

"Y'all's family has a chance to..."

Widow McClanon snarled and interrupted him. "We have supported y'all's fightn' enough. My late husband served. We've done our part."

Douglas stepped forward and held her hand. "Mother, it'll be alrigh'."

The Widow looked him in the eyes for a long hard moment. Then nodded slowly, she hugged him tightly. "Stay safe."

"I will." He held in his fear.

"Come home."

"I..." he blinked. "I will."

They both knew the truth. This could be the last time they would see each other. Even though they were not blood-related, this was the woman who'd raised him. He would miss her.

"Tell da others not ta worry." Douglas forced a smile. "I'll be back before they know it."

Widow McClanon squeezed him one last time before releasing him. "Goodbye, son."

Douglas turned to the soldier. He cleaned his glasses and walked out of the house onto the porch. "I'm ready."

The soldier didn't interrupt the moment.

He understood what the mother and son were feeling. William Loster had been drafted and forced to leave his wife with two infants. He was a small man with short wavy brown hair and dark brown eyes.

"The others are waiting down by the road. Got a horse?" William inquired.

"Yea. I can't take him tho, he belongs to da farm."

"We will leave one horse for the farm and take all the others." As William spoke this, two soldiers came from the barn leading Sizzle and the mule into the yard.

Douglas shook his head and took one last look at Widow McClanon. Her figure was silhouetted by the tall lamp behind her. He couldn't see her face.

"Alrigh' kid. Cmon."

Widow McClanon calmly shut the door as William led Douglas toward the rest of the group.

.....

Chapter Eight

Douglas counted forty-six men of various ages in the group, however most appeared to be in their mid-twenties. He recognized some of the local boys. They were huddled together, visibly worried and whispering.

His stubborn nature kept him from showing his anxiety. Widow McClanon had always said that the best way to be rid of fear is convincing yourself it doesn't exist.

William smiled with sympathy at the new recruit. "What's yer name, boy?"

"Douglas McClanon." He held out his hand and tried to look confident.

The soldier shook it. "I'm William Loster."

Douglas nodded. He made sure the wood ball was secure in his pocket. "Where are we headin'?"

"Up north to South Carolina."

"I've neva been outta Georgia."

Another soldier snickered, "Get used to it. You'll be travelin' now. That's if ya make it out of Sumter." A small group of soldiers chuckled in the darkness.

Douglas narrowed his eyes. "I thought we already had Sumter?"

"Yup. But somebody's gotta be there ta make sure them Union boys don't take it back. But don't worry, they'd be brash ta try it." William reassured him.

He nodded again and cleaned his glasses. *I should have said bye to Ellen and Sampson.*

His mind wandered back to his last moments with them.

What if I never see them again?

He touched the wooden ball in his pocket.

He hadn't seen Sizzle but knew he was in line somewhere with the other stolen horses from neighboring farms.

He toyed with the ball in his hand.

William tilted his head. "What's dat?"

Douglas flinched and shoved the ball back in his pocket not realizing it had been removed. "Nothin'." He adjusted his glasses. "When are we leavin'?"

William searched for an answer and wore a puzzled expression which reminded Douglas of Brick's face when there weren't enough food scraps in his dish. "Shoot. Don't really know.

We're waitin' on other recruits."

Douglas suspected the group would be starting the journey soon. Besides a couple of slowly dying cook fires, there were no signs of camping there for the night. It was clear when the others arrived, they would continue their march through the night.

.....

Douglas walked in the rear. He didn't trust anyone. His instincts were telling him that William was a good man, yet the whole experience was frightening. No matter how brave he tried to appear, he was still just a terrified kid. A farm boy.

Like the others in the group, he was familiar with long hours and hard work. Farm life had made him strong, so the hours of walking didn't tire him. If anything, it calmed him.

He noticed the Brooks boy in the middle of the group. Anger prickled in his chest but was quickly interrupted by someone banging into him from behind. Turning sharply, he saw it was a young drummer boy.

The boy could not have been older than twelve. He had shaggy hair, blue eyes, and his face was littered with freckles. "Sorry, sir." His accent was Georgian.

Douglas sighed at the kid. "Yer fine." He stretched his arms out above his head.

The boy had a crooked, toothy smile. "Yes, Sir."

Douglas chuckled, "I'm Douglas, not Sir. I'm Doug."

"Nice to meet ya." The boy nodded and walked beside him. "I'm Richard. But everybody calls me Rich."

Douglas yawned and poked the Rich's drum. "How long have ya been a drummer?"

Richard beamed at this attention. "Couple of months! I've never been in combat though. We're just recruitin' people on our way ta South Carolina." He softly rapped the drum. The hollow and eerie sound carried in the night.

Douglas glanced sideways at the dirty red-headed boy, and his protective instincts were awakened. He fidgeted with the ball in his pocket and spent the next few hours getting to know Richard.

.....

Chapter Nine

Douglas' thoughts were on the farm as he sat watching the flames flicker in the campfire. Every Friday night the family would have a campfire. The children would tell stories and play childhood games while catching fireflies until the stars filled the sky or until mama would rise from her porch rocker and declare bedtime. These were the happiest memories of his childhood.

Sampson would spend all week imagining the spookiest stories to tell. He enjoyed scaring everyone senseless. Not Ellen. She was immune to any type of fright. Neither was Widow McClanon afraid, instead, she'd correct his grammar.

Douglas forgot about his troubles for a short while. It was like being back at the farm, this pleasant feeling. It wasn't how he'd imagined his sixteenth birthday would be spent, in fact, it couldn't have been worse. He would give anything to be back home, sitting next to the family campfire's dancing flames.

However, if Mrs. McClanon had taught him anything it was that you had to adapt, stand up straight and never quit.

Douglas leaned against a tree. The sounds of tree frogs chirping sent him into a somewhat peaceful sleep as peaceful as it could be when miles away from home and headed to war.

. . . . .

That night his nightmare returned.

He was standing on the hill, watching the building burn. He tried to get a better look. But he knew it would be useless. His glasses were gone.

The dream went exactly as the time before. The shadowy figure told him to watch, but he refused.

The terrain wasn't like anywhere he had been before. It was a forest, but dry and less clustered with brambles and lush plant life.

Down the hill from where he stood, there was a ring of massive, flaming white trees. Their limbs hung proudly. Leaves were crinkling and turning to ash in the breeze. The trees surrounded the burning building like a crown of fire.

. . . . .

Chapter Ten

Six months had passed since the last dream. His company had arrived at Fort Sumter, and Douglas' life had eventually settled into a routine. The recruits had all heard horror stories from the battlefield, and it made Douglas grateful for his position as a guard.

Compared to his chores on the farm, this job was uneventful.

An advantage to guard duty was he had time to write letters home or what remained. Advancing companies had taken the majority of their livestock and stores. This enraged him, and by the letters he'd received, it infuriated Mrs. McClanon much more.

At this rate, the farm wouldn't produce the profits needed to keep the hired hands. In his letters, he offered Sampson advice. This was all he could do, but it didn't seem to make any difference. They needed him back, yet the only way he would return, was after his draft expired or in a casket.

Despite the troubling news of the farm, he enjoyed receiving letters. They were a necessary distraction. In his letters he refrained from talking about the war. He knew it would make them worry, and that was the last thing he wanted to do.

Douglas tossed the ball while sitting on his bunk. Supper was soon, and he needed time to prepare for the crowded mess hall. The noise and crowds still bothered him no matter how he tried to adjust.

William approached his bunk. "Hey, kid."

Startled, Douglas swiftly tucked the ball into his pocket.

William lifted an eyebrow. "Somethin' wrong? You look like you've seen a ghost."

"Ah…" He yawned and smiled at the older soldier. "Got a letter from home. They ain't doin' good."

William nodded in understanding and patted his shoulder. "Sorry to hear it. I'm sure they'll make it through fine."

He smiled slightly at the comforting gesture. William had become his army father.

The McClanons had never mentioned anything about his real mother and father. All Douglas knew was that he was better off without them. He had always thought Widow McClanon held a grudge against parents, but he never bothered to ask why. He didn't care. He had family, and for that he was grateful.

William drew him back to reality. "Think I hear the bell."

"Yea." He stood and followed William to the mess hall.

.....

The two sat at a table where Richard was entertaining the dining soldiers. They ate quietly, listening to the boisterous child spin tales of spirits and brave heroes of the Revolutionary War.

Richard leaped up on a stool as he finished his tale with exaggerated flourish and a voice lowered to a faint whisper. "Then the warlock burned the town to the ground." He made exaggerated motions and his voice faded dramatically.

Douglas chuckled while he ate watery stew and cornbread. He knew the story well. It was the tale of the marsh witch, a common legend taking place by the coast. It said that a necromancer settled at the edge of a village. The locals grew fearful of his power and plotted to murder him. Learning of their plans, the necromancer escaped and burned the village to ashes as he fled.

Of course, the story wasn't real. It was told to scare children into behaving. It was, however, useful entertainment when rallying morale. Everyone enjoyed a good fright.

William chuckled and finished his plate. "I've neva heard dat one."

"Really?" Douglas raised his eyebrows.

Richard finished his story and sat next to Douglas and William. "What did y'all think of that one?"

"Ya did good, kid."

Richard beamed with pride, highlighting his freckled cheeks. "Thank ya! My pop used ta tell us stories before bed."

Douglas was once again struck by how young Richard was. Too young to be away from home. And definitely too young for war. As if confirming his thoughts, Richard bounced up again and began spinning another yarn.

Douglas yawned and stretched his arms above his head. "I think imma head to bed."

"Doug! I was just getting to a good one!"

William gently pushed Richard's shoulder. "Let him go."

He put his plate in the wash tub and left for the bunkers. He preferred to hit the bunk early as his next post was at sunrise.

The standard issue socks had holes worn through them, which unfortunately had caused his feet to blister. Every step was followed by a quick jab of pain. It made him eager to retreat to the comfort of his bunk.

.....

Chapter Eleven

Two hours into his sleep, he was jarred awake by a dull booming noise. He immediately sat up, thinking it was a gun. His fears faded when he heard drunk laughter coming from outside.

"What the heck," he mumbled, still half asleep. No one else had awakened from the sound. He waited for a guard challenge the revelers but heard none.

Curious, he pulled on his trousers and searched for the source of the startling noise. As a precaution, he took a small pocketknife with him and quietly slipped out of the bunkhouse.

Just off to the west of his building, a few young soldiers were wobbling in his direction with whiskey bottles being passed between them. In the moonlight he could distinctly make out the Brooks boy. Even through the alcohol and bruises, he spotted him with his usual crew, staggering toward where Douglas stood in the shadow.

A couple of seconds of debating past when he decided to return to his bunk. The drunks would eventually be caught and punished for breaking curfew. He secretly hoped they'd be found by a commander. It would be nice to see Henry Brooks suffer after all the trouble he'd caused Sampson.

These unpleasant memories angered him, but Douglas forcefully set them aside and turned to the bunkhouse. Hearing the ruckus behind him, he gritted his teeth and kept walking. The sounds of the drunks' laughter only reassured him that this wasn't something worth fighting over.

At a good distance, they followed him to the bunkhouse, trying their best to walk upright. Douglas prepared himself for any trouble from the boys.

He heard a bottle crash against a wall and looked back over his shoulder. Henry had squared off with one of the other drunks. It was a boy Douglas didn't recognize. His mind was split between stepping in or walking on, when the Brooks boy swung the first blow. Douglas heard the punch connect with bone followed by the wet sounds of a bloody beating.

He followed his gut and continued. Someone else would find them and turn the lot in, and the boys would be put in the hold. Douglas hurried, lest he be caught up with them.

He was right in thinking that they would be caught, but wrong in thinking they would all be alive.

.....

He was sitting next to Richard in the dining hall getting the complete story.

"Rich, you're talkin' too fast. Start over."

"Okay!" Richard scooted in closer on his stool. "So, I heard from William, who heard from Johnson that Mark said-"

Douglas sighed and interrupted him. "Rich!"

"I'm sorry! Alright, two soldiers went missin' during the night. One was found dead on the beach rocks, and the other is still missin'."

"Missin'?"

"Or worse…." the boy whispered, "a boat is gone, too. Deserter."

Douglas choked on his drink. A small curse slipped out causing Richard to flinch and widen his eyes. "What's wrong?"

He set his tin cup down and coughed. "Nothin'." The lie rolled easily off his tongue. His curiosity once again forced him to ask. "Do ya know who da two missin' are?"

"Jefferson and Cain Jackson. The brothers."

"Alrigh'."

That means Brooks is still alive.

A smirk accidentally slipped over his features. He could get Henry in some trouble. This was quickly squelched, however, when he realized that the boy might also have seen him out that night.

I let them fight....

Did he notice me? What if he reports me instead?

I will be questioned. I would be implicated in the death!

Should I say something? Or just pray the drunks didn't notice me?

.....

An excruciatingly long guard duty passed in which Douglas was filled with dread over whether he'd been spotted by Brooks. Every passing officer seemed to be coming for him. Each time his name was called his breath would catch in his throat. Eventually, his shift was over, and it was clear that he wasn't going to be implicated in any of the trouble from the night before.

Douglas heard rumors, but he never found out what happened to the boys. It wouldn't be until his last day at Fort Sumter that he again saw Henry Brooks.

At the end of his duty, he went to his bunk, he kicked off his boots and opened the most recent letter from home. Douglas sat on his cot and carefully read it. Over many times. He heard Ellen's voice in the words. It was a much-needed distraction from his worry.

The soldiers seemed to have passed on from here. They have ceased ~~coming~~ raiding the farm, at least. We have just enough to make it through the next season. Do not worry about us. We will get on.

For happier news, Bird had a litter! Seven pups! We managed to sell a few. But mother says we can't feed them all. We can only keep two. I named one Flicker.

How is the war going up there? Have you seen any battles? Killed any Union? Sampson says not to ask. ~~He's such a sissy.~~
I'm praying for you, brother. Come home to us.
I hope to hear from you soon.
Your favorite sister, best friend, and fearless leader,
Ellen A. McClanon

Douglas folded the paper carefully and smiled. As always, Ellen's letter made him home-sick. He would feel it for a while. Missing home wasn't something that could be easily undone or unfelt.

.....

Chapter Twelve

Ellen,

I'm sorry I haven't written in a couple of months. The situation here has been rough. It is difficult to believe that it's been almost three years since I left home, but my draft will soon be over.

We received word that Union forces are coming this way. Looks like I might see combat after all. I hate that it's so close to my release.

I know what you're thinking, and no I'm not running. This place has become a home to me., and I'm prepared to defend it. Just remember that I'm also defending you, fearless leader.

Do me a favor and try not to worry

about it. They're just rumors after all. It's possible nothing will happen, and in a few months, I'll be back at the farm. It will be like I never left. Please look toward that.

Sorry to hear about Lizz. I pray she feels better. I'm praying for you all. Please continue to pray for me. It helps me to know you do.

Try not to get into too much trouble before I return. At least wait for me to help.
Your brother,
Douglas

.....

Three years. A thousand and ninety-five days. That's how long the draft lasted, and in a few months, he'll have reached the end of it. He'd be going home.

Douglas wondered how the farm had changed. It was frightening to think how much his family had also.

Will I even recognize them?

Will they recognize me?

Although he'd changed, the silver hair marked him still.

His nineteenth birthday was steadily approaching along with the end of his draft. He was now fully grown and shockingly tall, standing several inches above the tallest of men.

A much more significant change were his eyes. His eyesight was getting worse with each passing year. Douglas planned to have new glasses made when he returned to the farm.

His body was still strong, stronger even. It reassured him that he would be able to handle the bulk of chores when he got back as the hands had all been let go or drafted. The workload would be on Sampson and him.

.....

Douglas watched the waves from his post. Anxious officers stalked through the fort, barking orders. Recruits scuttled around wide-eyed. The general had brought in more troops in anticipation of a Union attack.

His gaze drifted to William, who was also taking his shift. In five weeks, he'd be leaving the fort and returning to his two children and wife.

Douglas was happy for him, but it was difficult to think about William leaving. He was his closest friend. Daily work would be a challenge without him.

Out of his peripheral he saw the soldiers coming for shift change. He gently nudged William in their direction. Douglas gave his replacement the rifle and followed William toward the mess hall.

"Heard anythin' from the family?" William asked.

Douglas shrugged, "Nothin' new. How 'bout you?"

William lit up at the mention of his family. "Kids and wife are well!"

"I'm happy for ya, Will."

"Yea. I can't wait to see 'em! But I'm worried the kids won't remember me."

Douglas snorted. "Of course, they'll remember you. You're their papa."

"Hope so. They were so young when I left 'em."

The conversation came to a brief halt when they heard a child laughing in the dining hall.

Richard must be telling a story.

William chuckled to himself as the two sat near the crowd that Richard was entertaining.

The drummer had run out of traditional stories long ago, so he'd invented new ones. And that day, Richard was telling one of his originals. It was the story of Ol' Man Dringin'.

"...then he jumped out of da bushes and growled at da travelers! They screamed an' he set his hogs after 'em!" Richard clanked his cup against the table to get everyone's attention, then ominously whispered, "The boys were never seen again."

Douglas was tucked into his food not bothering to pay attention. Richard saw this and purposely sat by him.

"What did ya like about that one?" he asked, knowing that Douglas hadn't been really paying attention. When Douglas hesitated, the boy laughed. "Ha! I knew ya weren't listenin'!"

William ruffled Richard's hair. "Why don't

ya tell him da whole story again, as punishment?"

"Whose side are ya on?" Douglas chuckled.

William shrugged as Richard prepared to tell the story for a second time. "Behind on old church lived-" But he was interrupted.

A soldier charged into the hall. Catching his breath, he yelled, "We're under attack! Stations!"

William shot out of his seat. Panic spread through the hall. It was hard to hear specific details over the stools scraping back from the tables and the den of a hundred questions from men racing to battle-ready positions. A bugle sounded the alarm from outside.

.....

Chapter Thirteen

Soldiers grabbed their rifles as officers shouted orders. This was what they had been repeatedly drilled, however, it was a mad scramble to get into position. William passed Douglas a rifle, and he frantically loaded it.

"Canon shot. They want ta scare us out. Shooting from da shore." William said calmly, but the panic in his eyes betrayed the calm reassurance.

Richard's eyes darted in fear. "Will they breach a hole in da wall?"

Douglas and William exchanged a glance. They both thought the same thing. There was no reason to worry him.

"We will shoot them before that happens." he lied.

Douglas double-checked his rifle. "Stay with me."

"O-okay."

William gave him a quick nod and went off to his position.

Douglas slung his rifle over his back and led Richard to where he was stationed. Since he was younger, he was instructed to stay farther back from the front lines, or in this case, stay inside the fort until the walls were breached.

Richard followed him stride for stride. He flinched every time a canon or gun went off, which became more frequent as the siege progressed.

A particularly loud boom shook the fort at its base. They could hear screams and an onslaught of gunfire.

Douglas suspected they were sending boats over filled with soldiers.

That must mean they are starting to penetrate the wall.

He gripped his rifle and crouched behind a barrel laying on its side in the corner. With shaking hands, he aimed for the corner ascertaining which direction the enemy would come by to seize this section of the fort.

Richard crouched beside him. He opened his mouth to say something, but Douglas stopped him with a warning look. They stayed behind the barrel for what felt like an eternity to the two young men. Occasionally they spotted one of their comrades. They could hear the battle and smell the smoke and powder. As of yet, no conflict had come their way.

Richard kept adjusting his sitting position. That aggravated Douglas slightly. He needed to concentrate. It was challenging enough to get a good aim with his poor eyesight. He didn't need Richard's fidgeting as an added distraction.

The screams slowly turned to yells as he heard soldiers coming their way. It didn't sound like a large group. He began to plan out what he and Rich should do. If he could get a few shots in, that would buy Richard enough time to escape towards a rear exit. And if they were lucky, a few boats might be tied up. They could hide under a tarp and possibly escape.

He remembered his written promise to Ellen. He had told her he would fight for this place. That is what he intended to do. And even as that thought passed, a Union soldier turned the corner. With the coldness of pure survival instinct, Douglas placed a bullet in the man's chest. Acrid smoke rolled up into his nostrils nearly choking him.

He gave this dead man no thought.

Giving Richard a quick pull up, he led him down the opposite way that led to a rear exit. This small gate led down to a fishing jetty behind the fort. Richard understood and ran while Douglas knocked barrels over to hinder anyone who might follow. He raced to catch up with the younger boy.

Gunsmoke fogged his vision so that his eyes were stinging, and tears ran down his cheeks. Just outside the exit, he saw Richard climbing into a two-person rowboat. There was no tarp or netting in the boat or laying alongside the jetty. This made escaping unseen riskier. He rushed over to help Rich.

"Hell!" Douglas cursed their bad luck. He said, "Rich, listen-"

"Are we gonna die-e?"

"No." He helped him settle into the boat. "Rich, you gotta do me a favor?"

"Yea-a." the boy was shaking and biting his lips so badly a bead of blood appeared on his bottom lip.

"I'm goin' back ta look for William-"

"No-o!" Richard's hands were trembling and his eyes blinked back tears. "No, stay with me!"

"Rich, ya have ta listen. I'm gonna push ya into da water. Lay flat on your back and don't move. Don't move, okay? Under no circumstances do ya look over da edge. At dark, get to rowing." He shoved oars into the boat. "Get as far as you can south. If you have to, swim to shore. Head south, then get home."

"Bu-ut da tide…"

"The current shouldn't be bad today. If you stay still, you'll be fine." Douglas began to untie the boat.

Richard nodded and laid flat in the boat. He was white from fear. The boy's wide eyes stared up at him.

Douglas heard people coming. He grabbed the leather ball from his pocket and shoved it into Richard's hand. "If ya ever get ta Savannah, bring this ta McClanon farms. They'll know what it means."

"Ok-kay."

Douglas smiled and squeezed his hand around the ball. "You'll be fine," he whispered, and then he gently pushed the boat into the waters. "Please God, get him home!"

.....

I'm going to die.
I'm going to die.
I'm going to die.

That is all he could think as he ran back down the corridors, smoke burning his eyes. Bodies were laying lifeless on the ground. Men and boys wearing both navy and tattered gray. He quietly ran in the direction of William's post.

Union soldiers were on the mainland firing the cannons. They were blowing the fort to pieces.

Coming around a storehouse, Douglas spotted a Union soldier. He fired and reloaded. No thought or emotion came to him. If he saw blue, he was shooting. That was all he could do.

A cannon blasted through the wall not

more than twenty feet behind him. He was instantly dazed by the explosion. A buzz and muted ringing filled his head. His eyes were stung by the dust.

Douglas quickened his pace as he neared William's post. It didn't seem possible, but there were more bodies here than in the hall. His gut turned when he saw the corpse of the Brooks boy laying half propped against a crumbling wall. His eyes were squeezed shut in pain and his hands were clasped holding his stomach from which blood soaked his dingy grey. Douglas paused wanting to do something, not knowing what.

He slipped through an exterior door that hung askew, dangling from its broken hinge. There were no living soldiers in the field.

Where are they?

Where'd they go?

His question was answered by the sound of a gunshot. He turned and saw a breach in the wall where a unit of Union soldiers were crouched in a sniper position.

Douglas saw them three seconds too late.

.....

Part Two

.....

Chapter Fourteen

His senses were useless. He struggled for even the slightest amount of feeling.

It felt like being asleep. Deep into a dream from which he could not awaken.

Trapped.

Yes.

That's the word.

Trapped.

.....

A ringing noise shot his conscious back into him.

What the hell-

Something was keeping him from moving.

Something is wrong.

He tried to draw in a breath and found his

lungs unwilling.

He tried to regain control of his body.

The ringing noise grew louder. Panic surged through him. The ringing was becoming unbearable.

Help!

He found his voice was without sound.

Breath came surging into him. He desperately, greedily gasped, filling his body with air. The more the ringing, the more his feelings returned.

After a few seconds, he gained control of his fingers and toes. Then his limbs, his head, and eventually his eyes. Sensations were traveling up his body causing painful tingling in his limbs.

His eyes popped open, and he was able to look around at his surroundings.

This isn't the fort.

Even without his glasses, he could tell that he was wrapped loosely in white fabric. He could move his limbs, but full motion was impeded by the stretch in the cloth. The pale light filtered into the confined space. He placed his hand against the white surface and pushed outward.

Douglas was stunned to hear muffled voices from beyond the white cloth.

What is this?

Did I die?

Where am I?

Unexpectedly the fabric opened, and he fell clumsily onto a hard floor. He yelled, frantically glancing around. His glasses were gone, making it difficult to get a good look at his surroundings. He was confused and disoriented.

The room had metal walls with no windows and bright white floors. Strange human-like forms loomed around him, quietly speaking and watching him. He noticed white cocoon shapes standing upright in rows.

The figures did not approach him. Nor did they speak. They seemed to be allowing him to orient.

Adapt to the situation.

He was wearing plain white pants and a shirt. The material was strange. He had never seen it.

Douglas slowly raised himself from his knees and uneasily stood. He tried to get a better look at where he was. A tall figure separated from the group and came to him. He spun Douglas roughly around and swiftly pulled his hands behind his back, throwing him off balance.

"Let me go! Who are you?" He screamed at the person, struggling to break free from the grip. His voice sounded hoarse and raspy to his ears. Panic was seizing his mind.

They did not respond.

His eyes narrowed at the other figures, squinting to see any details. As if he had been underwater before, his hearing suddenly became clear. The forms were speaking a language he couldn't understand.

Another figure broke off from the group and began approaching him. Terrified, Douglas yelled and tried kicking out. Trapped, he twisted to free himself but was roughly jerked back by the man behind him. The new person walked up to him and very gently placed his hands against Douglas' ears, strangely tapping them. His ears began to hum loudly. He could see the person's mouth moving but couldn't make out any sound. The hum then faded, and as it did, clarity came to him. He understood the person's words as if he had been born speaking this strange language or the figure had instantly learned English.

One female figure in blue clothing read off a clipboard. "Waker Eleven. Age of death, eighteen. Cause of death, a fatal gunshot wound to the chest. Half keeperial of slightly mixed genes. Half-human or possibly magus. Bad eyesight. Weak right leg." She looked up from the clipboard.

"What's goin' on?" Douglas growled loudly. An overwhelming terror seized him as the guard pushed him forward. "Get off me! Where am I?"

The female with the clipboard wrote something down and mumbled as Douglas was pushed onward. "Welcome, Waker Eleven, to the afterlife."

.....

He struggled to set his arms free from the guard's brutally tight grip.

Dead?

No! I can't be Dead!

The more he struggled the more the grip tightened.

"Take him to inspection." One of the strange, accented figures said coolly to the guard who was still holding. The guard responded with a curt nod.

Douglas' eyes widened and he stopped struggling. It was clear the guard had no intention of letting him go. His strength needed to be saved for whatever might come later.

The guard wouldn't relax his grip but pushed Douglas across the room and into the hallway. He took note of where he was being taken. Most of the walk was blurry to him, but he caught glimpses of rooms off the primary corridor.

He was being imprisoned, and his terror increased at this thought.

Did I do something wrong?

Is this hell?

The guard walked him down a hallway of what appeared to be hospital rooms. A door to one was opened, and he was shoved inside. Douglas crashed into a metal cot. The door was slammed shut and locked.

What is happening?

His heart drummed dangerously wild in

his chest. He banged his hands against the door. In his racing mind, walls came suddenly together, making him feel tight and closed in.

"Let me out!"

An image from his past came vividly to him. A time when he was gathering eggs from the chicken coop, Sampson had locked him in as a joke. Douglas had learned of his fear that day. Fear of being closed in, trapped. That had been the most terrifying experience of Douglas's childhood. Small, enclosed spaces made his breath short and his mind spin.

He pounded his fists on the door. He was at the point of despair and near giving up hope that someone would come when the door abruptly opened, knocking him to the floor. It was the female person with the clipboard.

The person chuckled and heaved him up. "New Wakers. They are very amusing."

Douglas smacked her hand away. "Wakers? Who are you? What's this all about?"

"Yes, Wakers. The new nephilim that wake up."

Douglass shook his head in confusion. "Nephilim?"

This time she didn't respond. She looked at her clipboard and made a notation. "Waker Eleven. Hmm. It says you have bad vision?"

Breathing deeply, Douglas nodded and tried to calm down. His mind was racing to find a reason behind it all, but nothing came.

What's a nephilim?
What is this place?

The lady scribbled something more. "Interesting. Nephilim usually have advanced senses. I don't think I've ever seen one that required glasses."

"Please," he begged, "tell me what I am doing here? What is a nephilim? Why am I being held here?"

The inspector once again wouldn't answer his questions. Instead, she continued writing on her clipboard. "There is an advanced healing method that might work for your eyesight. But it has risks." She shook her head. "No. Your blood type would not respond appropriately. Shame."

"Can't I just get a new pair of glasses?" Douglas took a mental note that she refused to answer his questions. He did not understand what she was talking about.

Advanced healing methods?

"No one here has glasses. You're the first one who has ever needed them...that I know of."

Douglas sat on the edge of the cot and ran his hands over his face, trying to find some explanation.

Was this a dream?

He kept coming back to the same conclusion. Some facts were beginning to come to him, and thoughts were moving into place like a jigsaw puzzle. He whispered almost to himself, "So this is heaven...or hell. I have died."

"Correct. Hazdrim, to be exact."

"Hazdrim?" He did not remember this from the Widow's Bible readings. "Is that the good or bad place?"

"It's er-" She paused and tapped her pencil against the clipboard. "-complicated."

"Complicated?" He felt his gut sink.

"They'll explain it later. After your exam is finished."

"Can't ya just lemme go? It's been a long... actually how long has it been?"

"I'm sorry, I'm not allowed to divulge information." She pulled a metal syringe out of her bag. "Now, I need to get a blood sample."

His hand involuntarily shot to his pocket only to find that the ball was not there. Panic to surged through his veins.

"No. No. No." He backed away slowly. "No one is gettin' my blood unless I receive an explanation." His fists tightened.

The 'doctor' swallowed, eyeing him. This Waker was extremely tall. One of the largest she had seen.

The lady was significantly smaller than him, and Douglas was confident that he could hold his ground against her.

She spoke calmly as if to a child. "I know that this is all confusing...hard to comprehend. Realizing you've passed on. It is a lot to take in. Unfortunately, I'm not allowed to tell you anything at the time being. I'm sorry, you'll have to wait."

Her tone aggravated him significantly, but after a few seconds of debating his options, he decided to let her take the blood. He rolled up his sleeve and looked away.

The doctor nodded and grabbed the needle. She pricked a vein in his arm and the syringe began filling with his blood.

Douglas flinched when she was done and frowned as she cleaned it thoroughly. "Why do you need my blood?"

"Just to gather some information about your genealogy."

"Oh. Is dat important in hell?"

"Well, yes. We need to know what percentage of you is keeperial."

Douglas narrowed his eyes. "Keeperial?"

The doctor scrunched up her face and shook her head. "I shouldn't have said that." She wrote a few more notes and hurried over to the door. "I'll return shortly."

.....

Chapter Fifteen

The white shirt scratched against him uncomfortably. His skin seemed to be overly sensitive to the simple cotton shirt.

The doctor had left, and Douglas was trying to get a better grip of the situation.

Everything appears to function like the real world.
But something is different.
This doesn't feel like the 'Heaven and Hell' from church.
It's less majestic or demented.
This place is all sterile and white and too shiny.

The sound of a turning doorknob grabbed his attention. He heaved himself up and leaned against the wall.

The doctor from earlier entered. She sighed. "I hate this part."

"What? You...you hate this part?" He held his hands up. "I hate bein' told I'm dead an' forced to give ma blood. I don't have my glasses. And all this blurry movement is givin' me a headache." His anger surprised him.

Mrs. McClanon wouldn't appreciate his outburst at all. She did not tolerate tantrums. She had always insisted that he control his emotions. Especially his anger. It tugged at his memories. For the first time, the finality of his circumstances struck him hard.

I'm really dead.

I'll never see The Widow again.

Or Sampson.

Or the girls.

This new reality scared him. At first, he'd been so panicked that he couldn't properly take it in, but now he had no choice. He had to focus. Who knew what other information was coming? Based on the fact that they needed blood tests and were waiting to release this information...he imagined something must be wrong.

"I'm sorry. This whole...thing is just confusing. I want to know where I am." He tried to sound calm and non-threatening.

"I understand." The doctor nodded. "The simplified version is that humans aren't the only creatures on earth. There are other creatures called Keepers who bred with humans while they were active on earth. Many years ago. Their offspring are not human. Therefore, they can't go on to the human afterlife. Heaven or hell, you call it. Everyone sent here is at least a certain percentage of keeperial."

"Alrigh'." A hundred questions flooded his mind. This wasn't the explanation he was expecting. The information wasn't comforting, but not nearly as bad as being in hell. "Keeperial? What are they?"

"They inspired the human theories of ghosts, many gods, angels, and demons. Only five Keepers have lived in our realm. Their descendants," she explained, nodding at him, "have been known to possess some of their characteristics. This is why we do the blood tests. I assume your genetics is probably strong." She gestured to his hair. "Silver hair, unusual skin tone. Your height."

"No one here is human?"

"No. Everyone here is partially human, but the keeperial gene is dominant. This is why we come here when we die."

"But we aren't angels...or demons?"

She chuckled, "Oh dear, no. They are different."

He nodded and rubbed his forehead. "When do ya get da blood test thin' back."

"They are testing the samples now. We just do tests to see how much keeperial blood you have. And if we can, show how much of their traits you possess."

"What are da traits?"

"Abhuman strength, durability, and the ability to make 'casts' which are effectively spiritual weapons."

Spiritual weapons?

Weapons for what?

"So, these Keepers mated with humans?" He asked, making eye contact. "And dat makes nephilim?"

The doctor didn't return his gaze but focused on her clipboard while responding. "Keeper mixed with humans. Sometimes there is the alternate magus gene. However, nephilim-magus is rare. You'll learn more later."

.....

Douglas was shown a map of the Hazdrim territories or regions. The word region, he learned, was used in reference to land guarded and governed by unique tribes of soldiers.

There were five regions. Five tribes. Each one was dedicated to a known Keeper. The Wakers would have the opportunity to choose the region they would call home. Having just "woken" and not knowing about the territories' particular problems, the process of choosing a home felt more random than Douglas would've liked. It made him feel helpless.

Douglas paced around the hospital room trying to decide between the two regions. One was secluded. It was a land of fertile valleys and coastal islands. The other was known for its strength and aggressive power. It was a land of thick forests and woodlands.

The helpers informed him that he would receive one night to stay and regain his strength. Tomorrow he would need to decide where he wanted to go. They would take him to his new home. He felt rushed and uneasy about how quickly it all was happening. But Douglas had learned in the war that fear could be conquered. Control over his emotions would be an asset that would serve him.

The hospital-like building was centrally located on the border between all five regions. It was called the Waking Center. Official representatives from each region were sent to assist with the Waking and bring their new Wakers home.

After some time, he received food and water. Unfamiliar meat was on the plate. He inspected it carefully before eating. It was chewy and plain and didn't taste like anything he'd eaten before. It wasn't pork, beef, or venison. But his appetite was returning, so he was happy to have it.

Douglas took careful bites, letting his mind replay the strange events that had taken place.

The region that sparked his interest the most was Tavdren. They had closer communities, it was secure, and their soldiers were said to be invincible in battle. They were warriors. He felt instinctively drawn to this powerful territory. The idea of might, dominance, and control was suddenly compelling. This had never been on his heart before, and he wasn't sure where it was coming from. Instinct was all he had at the moment. And instinct told him to value power and safety rather than simple comfort.

Comfort doesn't last.

The doorknob turned and the doctor walked in. "It is time to go. The last step is choosing a region and a name."

"I already have a name."

"Most nephilim chose new ones. It helps them feel like they are getting a new start. I recommend something personal."

Douglas nodded. He couldn't explain it, but he was feeling less like Douglas the longer he was in this other world. Choosing a new identity wasn't an uncomfortable idea. He even welcomed it.

He thought for a while before making a decision. "I will go to Tavdren. And I will be known as Moccasin Clanon." Moccasin, after the time he saved Sampson from the water snake. Clanon, after the McClanons. This way he would always have pieces of his life on earth.

The doctor nodded and made a notation. "Tavdren? This is your choice?"

"Yea...why...is there somethin' wrong?"

"No." She forced a smile.

"Yea..." Douglas, now Moccasin, pushed his plate away. "When do we leave?" He was eager to get on with the rest of his life here.

"In twenty minutes. You will be given sixty foald, our currency, and an assignment by your guide. Your assignments are temporary and based upon our preliminary assessment of your character."

Before he could ask anything further, she announced. "That is all. Your guide will advise you on the route." Then she was gone.

.....

A tall woman in red armor was guiding the Tavdren Wakers out of the building. He couldn't make out many details of her because his eyesight was so poor, but his impression was the color red. She had a commanding presence that was without question. Moccasin hadn't been surprised to find others like himself gathered around her in the departure area. She had a heavily accented voice and was explaining Tavdren as they began their long hike to the region.

Overhead, the sky was already dark navy and purple, lit by a large orange moon. The environment outside appeared frozen in time. Beautiful, but hauntingly so. Moccasin was in awe of this new world which bore similarities to earth yet was unique.

The Wakers walked in silence, listening to their guide. The forest was rolling and became thicker making the path difficult at times to pass. The moon lit up their surroundings in an enchanting, pale orange light.

Their guide provided information at such a rapid pace, so that it was hard to keep up with what she was saying. He found it challenging to absorb it all.

Moccasin walked close. He wanted to learn as much as possible about his new home. "The Keeper dat it's based on, will we see him?"

"Tavdren is based on the Keeper, Tavious, hence our liking to forts." This prompted muffled laughter from the experienced soldiers who traveled with her. Moccasin didn't understand the jest. "No one has seen the five Keepers since they died a second time here. Several thousand years ago."

Died a second time!

A second death was possible?

Moccasin adjusted his shirt collar. It was becoming achingly uncomfortable. "Will I be assigned a job, or do I choose?"

"I recommend joining the force as I did. It pays well, but the perks are worth more than foald." She tossed a small dagger in the air. "We're always looking for recruits. You're a big guy. You'll do well."

"I don't know...servin' is how I died." He stumbled over a tree root.

"You have time to decide, but you would like life at the fort. Your fellow soldiers become family. It's nice." The woman held her hand out. "I'm a highrindh. You will call me Highrindh Bera." Her fingertips glowed red. Moccasin suspected it was a sign of her keeperial blood. He was curious but didn't want to ask her.

Moccasin shook her hand. "I'm Dou-Moc-casin." He smiled, openly. Even though he couldn't really see her clearly, he could tell she was dangerous, and not someone he wanted as his enemy. "I'm familiar with military life."

"All the better. Welcome to hell, Mocca-sin." Bera slipped the dagger into its sheath. "How was your waking?"

Moccasin shrugged and stumbled on a root. He quickly caught himself. "It could have been better. Bit of a shock, ya know. What is a highrindh?"

"It is my title. I am a general, one of three. I believe that is your word for it."

Hesitantly, he asked, "They told me that this ain't hell. Is this hell?"

"When you are here for as long as I, it mat-ters not."

A cloud covered the moon for a few sec-onds. It made the forest cease its vibrant color-ing.

"Does the sky ever change?"

"Like earth, a sun replaces the moon dur-ing the day." Bera looked up at the full moon.

Moccasin rubbed his forehead. He needed a pair of glasses. "Would ya know of a place dat makes glasses?"

Bera looked puzzled. "Glasses? What are those?"

"Dey help with eyesight. You don't know..." he squinted at her face. "Exactly how long have ya been here?"

"Hm..." She narrowed her eyes in thought. "...a few hundred years. I stopped caring."

"Dang. I thought ya could die here."

"You can, but our bodies don't age as on earth. With some assistance, you won't ever die from old age."

"Immortality?" His gut dropped.

"Not necessarily. Like I said, with assistance you can age up or down. It's a simple spell." She held a hand up. It glowed flame red again. "But it's very draining."

Moccasin stared at her hand. He held back the temptation to get a better look. "How do you do that?"

Bera shrugged. "Only certain nephilim can do casts. The ones that are closely related to the keepers." She tilted her head. "You look like you'd be able to wield it. Because of your-"

"Hair and eyes."

"Yes, and your size." She waved her hand across the night sky. "It's shocking at first, but you'll soon accept the fact that you're not human and embrace it."

.....

Chapter Sixteen

Bera led the group through a dry birch forest. Leaves crackled underfoot and in places obscured their way. Thinly covered roots rose as treacherous obstacles. Moccasin found the path to be laborious and slow going, causing him to secretly question their guide.

A few Wakers at a time were given papers and held quiet conversations with Bera. These few would then pull away from the group to begin their assignments and their own afterlives in villages they passed. Gradually the company was growing thinner.

Moccasin had not received his assignment. He wondered if he would be going to the 'fort' with Bera. He understood the assignments were simply to help with the Waker's transition, but he felt compelled to stay at the fort if that was his job. There was still a risk in joining the soldiers, but he was familiar with that life and that itself was comforting.

"Last village until the fort." Bera informed those remaining. She gathered all but six and gave them their work orders. They, like all the others before, strayed away through a town gate.

Moccasin watched the last of the Wakers enter the ancient stone walls. Bera, him, and the last six nephilim were left.

"You all will come with me."

Her statement startled him. "I see."

"You will be given jobs inside the fort if you desire to stay and join."

"I'll join. I can do that. I have done that. Before..."

"Excellent!" Bera patted his shoulder. "Every Waker, or recruit, has to be mentored in our ways, then there's an initiation."

"What initiation?"

"Secret. We like the element of surprise. It's more fun to watch this way."

"Watch?"

Bera grinned, mischievously. "You'll see when the time comes."

The grin sent a shiver down his spine. He instantly feared the initiation. Bera seemed like the kind of nephilim who enjoyed the gruesome. *It can't be that bad.*

.....

They made camp for the night. It was a

challenge getting settled as the bright moon cast shadows among them. He couldn't shut his mind off and get to sleep in this bizarre new world. The cool forest was not as calming as the sultry Georgian woods.

Moccasin doubted that it would ever be the same.

How could it?

As if confirming his fears, a cold feeling burst into him. A startling, icy blast. His eyes darted around the foggy trees. He squinted all around the blurry perimeter of camp where the campfire's light flickered on the trees. His eyes caught the gaze of another. He felt danger emanating from it, but most alarming was the pure white cloth. The familiar white figure from the farm. It felt as if his dream from years ago was becoming real in this place.

Once again, his hand reached inside his empty pocket and began to tremor to when it didn't find the comforting touch of the ball. Panic began to rise, but he held it. The figure was now close enough for him to be sure that it was a person.

I wasn't imagining it!

It's followed me here!

It hadn't harmed him on earth, perhaps it wouldn't here.

Moccasin imagined that he heard whispering coming from the figure. He remembered the sound of it from his dreams. The whispering grew louder, and it took all his strength not to look away from the terror in its eyes.

Whatever this is...

It must be related to something here.

That can't be good.

.....

The morning came with clear blue skies and bright sunshine. Somehow, he had fallen asleep, staring at the spot where the phantom had faded into a mist. Moccasin hadn't told Bera about the white shape. She was focused on getting them to the fort as soon as possible, and it was clear Bera was not a person who would tolerate distractions.

She elaborated on understanding the casting process. "The key is to resist overthinking. Casting doesn't come from your thoughts. It comes from inside." She punched him in the stomach for emphasis. "That is if you have enough keeprial blood to cast. Which I'm sure you do. The only way to do it successfully at first is by telling yourself you can. Doubt has consumed many strong blooded nephilim."

"Got it." The fort was within half a day's journey, and he found he was anxious for this new life, even though the more rational part of him was filled with many unanswered questions.

Bera leaped over a fallen branch. The others followed her. "Only a few hours till we reach the fort! Remember what I told you. Have confidence and don't ever be caught reading."

Moccasin chuckled, thinking this was a joke, however, a loathing scowl from Bera told him otherwise. "I was just laughing at the idea of anyone reading."

The highrindh was satisfied by that answer.

.....

Chapter Seventeen

Atticus Coral, the leader of Tavdren's group of defenders, was easily the best known nilaon in all the regions. His aggression and raw ambition were well known in a short amount of time.

His fort was just as intimidating. It was a massive fortress made of cold, dark grey stone. The structure was secluded deep in the foggy birch forest, hidden from view. They came upon it unexpectedly as it seemed to have simply materialized from the forest as if it was protected by the trees and mist. Or was a part of them.

Moccasin could see that the thick walls were shot with tiny windows which would allow only the faintest bit of dull light to seep inside. He saw men upon the walls of the two rounded towers. It was a castle fort from picture books he'd seen in the schoolhouse in Waller, Georgia.

Bera had called it a fort, but the stone carvings covering the exterior walls made him wonder if there was more to the place than military defense. Moccasin had never seen anything more disturbingly beautiful before. He walked close to Bera as they entered through the massive wooden doors. His instincts told him that the group was being watched as they passed through into the dark entrance hall. It was an empty space with a plethora of mounts hanging above as decoration.

The other Wakers were also aware of being watched and were visibly concerned. That encouraged Moccasin to hide his budding fears. From what Bera explained, if Nilaon Atticus could sense fear, it would not go well for the recruit. Hiding his emotions help him stand apart from the other nervous Wakers.

"This way." Bera tapped on a door. Her fingertips glowed red as she drew a symbol on it.

The door opened to reveal a courtroom where a hundred or more people were chatting and casually watching the throne. They seemed to be awaiting the person who claims it.

No one bothered to engage Bera's group of Wakers. The gathered soldiers cast contemptuous, sideways glances as they passed, reminding Moccasin of the school yard when the older boys picked on the younger. He had the impression they were sizing up the new kids. It frustrated him, the poor way the Wakers had been treated from the beginning. He resented information being sprung on him, being forced to make decisions without time to consider his options properly and then being abruptly pushed from the Waking Center.

His train of thought was swiftly interrupted by Bera. She left the group and hurried over to another nephilim. "Gashly, what did I miss?"

In the lighting, Moccasin noticed for the first time that Bera had long, red hair that fell loose down her back. She was as tall as her male peers and striking.

Moccasin's gaze wondered about the courtroom, taking it all in. Statues of warriors, animals, gargoyles, along with mounts of unknown creatures decorated the throne. Without the crowd, the room could be considered grotesque. Moccasin couldn't see the nephilim well, but he could tell they were all soldiers by their mannerisms. Every eye appeared full of calculation with questionable intentions.

"Attention!" A voice rumbled.

All chatter immediately fell and everyone in unison turned to the source. In walked a large nephilim with what looked to Moccasin like a grey and brown fox cape over his armor. He addressed the crowd.

"Highrindh Bera has returned from The Waking, bringing with her forty civilians and six potential soldiers. Per Nilaon Atticus' request, I will take his place in assigning their consultants. My fellow highrindh will assist if they wish."

Bera nodded her head. "I assume I will have first pick?"

"Of course, as guide you will." He turned to another figure. "And Highrindh Jin?"

The second highrindh was a young female with long, straight black hair. She was smaller than Bera but had a large presence and a commanding voice. She was wearing a hooded covering over grey and rose-colored armor. It was clear to Moccasin that Jin wasn't pleased with Atticus' absence. "I don't mind you deciding for the others, but like Highrindh Bera, I expect to have my pick."

The fur caped man nodded to Bera and the highrindh called Jin. Moccasin felt the tension between the three highrindh. There was a clear hostility between them. "Of course. The six Wakers who wish to join, step up."

Moccasin took the first step. He approached the man, trying to hide any emotion. His fellow Wakers followed. It surprised him that he didn't care what the others did. Now was the time to care only about himself. He met the male highrindh's gaze and held it. The man seemed curious by the act, as Moccasin had intended. This confidence was new, and he was pleased to feel it growing.

Bera and Jin stepped up next. Bera pointed

at Moccasin. "I'll take that one."

The armored man nodded. "Fine. High-rindh Jin?"

"That one." She said without a moment hesitation, pointing a long finger at a Waker.

Moccasin narrowed his eyes. He had an instant dislike of Jin, although he had no idea where it came from.

The male highrindh made his pick and assigned the other Wakers to their consultants.

.....

Chapter Eighteen

A week had passed, in which Moccasin found Bera to be a dedicated consultant. She'd taught him how to do simple casts. A cast, he discovered, was an energy that could be used for attacking or defending. It could be shaped for whatever purpose was required. Only nephilim with purer Keeper blood relations had this ability, and those with the highest keeperial blood had the strongest casting. Casts were manifested as different colors depending on the nephilim. Bera had realized early on in their journey from the Waking Center that Moccasin had this trait, which is why she chose him. His casting was silver.

Hers was red.

The white vision that had haunted his dreams had become a frequent visitor. Understanding the mysterious dream phantom wasn't something he could manage. His training required all of his attention; therefore, he strove to ignore the white mist. As long as it remained elusive and harmless, his priority was to pass the Tavdren initiation and integrate into their fierce, warrior culture.

Each recruit had received a small room in the fortress. His room contained a bed and a small table with an oil lamp. There was a chest at the foot of the bed for storage. He had a slit for a window. Bathing and dining facilities were located at the end corridor. For the first three days, he had trouble navigating the maze-like hallways. This was in part due to his own ignorance but was primarily the fault of Tavdren soldiers who gave intentionally false directions.

The three highrindh and Atticus, each had a suite of rooms off a third-level corridor. Moccasin had yet to lay eyes on their leader. If he was completely uninterested in meeting the recruits or had more urgent matters, Moccasin didn't know. He'd gleaned, however, that it was uncharacteristic for their nilaon to be absent during the first week of training.

Moccasin heard knocking on his door while he was dressing for the day. He hadn't been given any armor yet, just trousers and a shirt in a very heavy, durable material.

He opened the door halfway. "Hello?"

"Moccasin!" Bera pushed the door in and slapped his shoulders in greeting. "I see you're already dressed for training! Excellent! We've got a long day ahead of us! Let's go!" She pulled him out into the hallway.

"Ow!" Moccasin's shoulder banged against the door.

Bera rolled her eyes. "Don't worry, I've got someone working on your 'glasses'." She snorted and Moccasin could have easily mistaken her for a dragon breathing hot air.

"Really? Thank you."

"Seems unnecessary, but whatever keeps you from embarrassing me at your initiation." Her walking was at such a fast pace that he struggled to keep up while hopping into his left boot. "We'll age you today. That should fix your clumsiness and increase your casting abilities."

"Alright..." He dodged a corner while rolling up his sleeves. "How old will you age me?"

"Hmm." Bera directed him down a staircase. "Nephilim are strongest between their twenties and fifties. Preferably twenties for you, unless you want to be an older man." She punched his bicep, but he ducked, only to be met with another well-aimed blow to his already bruised shoulder.

"Just a few years, then?" He asked, his eyes landing on Bera's death scar.

A death scar was the mark of a nephilim's demise. The gunshots that killed him left purple and black scars on his chest and his right earlobe. Bera for instance had been decapitated. Moccasin could see the jagged scar across her neck. It was an unspoken rule not to inquire about a nephilim's cause of death or death scar, yet he was certain she had a gruesome death tale.

Bera lead him out of the building and into a dirt field in the rear of the fort. Daily training was conducted outside in the courtyard or the nearby field. On days with inclement weather, training took place in a large open chamber where a ring had been constructed.

"Show me a simple cast." Her heavy Norse accent flashed briefly.

Moccasin nodded and held out his dominant left hand. A small silver spark appeared from his index finger.

Bera smiled encouragingly, but he didn't share her excitement at all. Everything happened at fast clip in Hazdrim. His earthly sentiments were fading as the days passed.

He tried another cast, focusing on a shield image she'd taught him the previous afternoon. And then instantly, the white vision materialized behind Bera. Moccasin faltered and the silver shield cast vanished abruptly.
It's back.

"Focus!" Bera shouted, bringing him to attention.

Bera had told him of a creature like similar to nephilim, called the magus. Unlike nephilim, who could inherit the keeperial tool of casting, a magus could manipulate sensory perception with incantations. Magus could trick the mind, but not cause physical damage.

Magus and nephilim had mated, creating a powerful race of nephilim-magus. They were rare in the realm and immensely feared by Nephilim because, Bera explained, the combination of powers was well beyond the typical nephilim.

The two continued casting. Working through offensive positions, and Bera seemed pleased with his natural abilities. "Good. Now, prepare to defend yourself."

"What?"

Bera smirked and landed an uppercut that sent him falling to the ground with a thud. "Like I said..." Bera's fingers glowed red. The red sparks formed a shield shape. "...defend yourself."

She hoisted him to his feet. "Casting can save your life in battle. For a nephilim, casting is a blessing." She clenched her fist together and smacked him with her red shield. "Now...defend yourself."

Moccasin rubbed his cheek. He planted his feet and summoned a few silver sparks that twisted slowly into a shield. It wasn't as perfect as Bera's. Her casting was fluid and elegant from years of honing, while his was still static and inconsistent.

Bera focused her attention on the moment. She stepped forward and kicked at his side. He ducked and swung up a blotchy shield-cast. The shields clashed loudly. This seemed to anger her. She lunged and spun a round kick, yet he managed to side-step away.

"Bera!" A voice interrupted the skirmish. "I have the tool you requested!" A young nephilim approached and pulled a case out of a canvas bag.

Bera's fierce, combat-ready features were quickly replaced by a warm smile. "Thank you."

Breathing heavily, Moccasin stretched to regain himself. The silver sparks faded out of sight and back into his fingers. "What's that?" He panted.

"Your bizarre seeing glass tool."

"Thank goodness!" He smiled and reached for the case.

Tavdren armorers were naturally talented, but he hadn't expected the glasses to be this well-crafted. They were bronze and perfectly fitted to his face. The lenses were crystal and enhanced his eyesight more than his earthly pair.

"Are you pleased with them?" Bera asked, watching him look around at his world clearly for the first time.

He smiled widely, taking a good look at Bera for once. "Thank you!" The 'death-scar' on her neck stood out dramatically. In fact, the glasses revealed a few tiny, white scars on her face and neck. Her bright red eyes were not as frightening as he'd expected but were instead warm with a mischievous twinkle. At that moment, with her shield-cast blazing, her eyes were bright red, but he could see brown flecks that came forward as her cast faded from her fingertips. She had a lovely face despite the scars.

Bera smiled at him and held out two fingers. "Can you see?"

He rolled his eyes and pushed her fingers away from his face. "I could always see. It was just blurry."

"If you say so." She tapped his glasses. "I'll have a few more pairs made because I'll inevitably break them."

.....

Chapter Nineteen

Moccasin stood looking at himself in a mirror, and a grown man stared back at him.

The aging process had been an amber colored potion made by a healer physician that once consumed, drew him into a deep sleep. He found himself waking up in the late evening still very drowsy and with stiff, sore joints and muscles. The metamorphosis from his eighteen-year-old body into a twenty-three-year-old revealed a striking difference. Not only had his facial features sharpened, but his neck and shoulders had transformed into thicker, more rounded versions of their prior state. Examination of his arms and legs revealed the same changes. He wasn't any taller, having already reached his full height, but there was more mass to his limbs.

The purpose of taking the aging drought hadn't been to alter his appearance, but to advance his casting ability. And it did. His casting exponentially improved with his increased age, making him stronger and more confident.

"Moccasin?" Bera's voice asked from outside of his room. "I need to see how well the aging worked. Don't worry if you have multiple heads. We can fix that."

"Ha!" he laughed, "Yeah, I'm ready." He tapped his ear. He had not noticed it before, but there was a small tear in his ear from where one Union bullets had grazed him. It must have closed up when he awoke here, but the aging had reopened the wound.

He opened the door and slammed into her as she barreled inside.

"Well, you're still clumsy, but at least now you can withstand a cast beating." She picked up his hand and made the casting gesture. "The initiation is in a few days. You need to keep working."

Moccasin nodded and summoned a small cast. A silver sphere shaped like his old wooden ball from earth.

"So, the initiation..."

"Sorry. You know I can't tell you anything."

"Can ya just tell me if it's dangerous?"

Bera rolled her eyes. "Of course, it is,

idiot! How do you think I got this?" She made a swooshing gesture to a tiny scar on her cheek. "You'll be lucky if you manage to make it out with eight fingers."

"That's not very-."

"Eh, you'll be fine." She punched his shoulder.

"Your version of 'fine' ain't very comfortin'," Moccasin drawled.

Bera made mocking gestures. "Maybe, but you'll find out one way or the other." She turned and whisked out of his room.

Moccasin watched her leave. "Good nigh'." He pushed the glasses higher up his nose and closed the door. He thought that he would never get used to Bera's spontaneity, and yet something in her odd mixture of infuriating and fun reminded him of Ellen.

Leaning against the back of the door, he smiled at a memory of his younger sister.

.....

The next morning, after a full day and night of rest, he'd awoken early and was on the field at dawn. No one but the tower guards were present, allowing him some quiet practice.

Focus on the target.

A stump was set up in a ditch. He summoned the saber-cast.

Concentrate.

Moccasin took a deep breath and swung a saber-cast at the stump. His saber-cast managed to hold up, causing a slash to appear in the wood.

"Better." He mumbled to himself while setting the stump back in place. The process was repeated a few more times.

"You're doing better." The sharp voice of Highrindh Jin rattled him. He turned swiftly to her. With his concentration broken the cast re-absorbed into his fingertips.

Jin's face was tight and sharp, making her expressions appear as a snarl. Her eyes were bright pink, similar to her casting color.

"Thank you," Moccasin mumbled. "May I help you with anything?"

"The Waker's blood tests arrived last night. Bera is feeling ill and asked me to speak with you."

"I see." He looked past her shoulder, to the fortress. He doubted that Bera wasn't well.
Why does Jin lie?

Cautiously, he asked her, "Where are they?"

"Bera's office." Jin was emotionless. "As a highrindh, we get to see the tests." Her eyes narrowed on his death-wound, causing him to feel uncomfortable.

"You've seen mine?"

Jin nodded, still staring at him.

His instincts told him not to trust Jin. She was a person who did everything for personal gain, and something was rumbling deep inside of him that had an instant contempt for her. A growing hatred.

Jin shrugged. "Atticus will want to speak with you." A cautious smile grew across her face. "After all, it isn't every day that we see a nephilim-magus."

Moccasin's eyes widened at hearing her accuse him of having the magus gene, but he quickly reined his emotions. "I will go to him, now."

He didn't believe her and wondered why she'd lie. Jin reminded him of the Brooks boy. Always looking for trouble.

Jin's smile vanished. Obviously, this wasn't the reaction she had anticipated. "Magus have a reputation for being rebellious. The only other nephilim-magus in the region is imprisoned in our dungeon."

This worried Moccasin, but he wouldn't let her know. He could see she was trying to pull it out of him. "Even if I am truly a magus, why should that make any difference?"

He walked past her and headed in the direction of the castle.

Jin snarled. "Listen-"

"No. You listen." Throwing caution aside, Moccasin swung back around to face the high-rindh. A voice of authority came from him. "I know what you're doing, and I know who you are." He didn't understand where it came from; it just welled up from somewhere buried inside. His gut was telling him to push back against this highrindh.

Jin was startled at his impertinence. She opened up her mouth to reply, but again, he cut her off. "Enjoy your afternoon, Highrindh."

There were consequences for his tone. No Tavdren soldier challenged a highrindh as he had and not received punishment. Bera reprimanded him and made it clear that had she not intervened he would've faced a much harsher penalty. He was put on the night shift guarding the cold dungeons for five days.

. . . . .

Jin was correct in saying that Atticus would request to see him. He did. Right away. That was the first warning sign.

Ultimately, Moccasin wasn't as concerned about being part magus as he was finally meeting the nilaon. He was a nephilim, yet the idea of being a magus, or mage, was interesting. It meant he could potentially have access to new abilities. Rare power. He could see this as being useful, however for the present, being accepted was more important than gaining power.

He made his way toward Atticus' study. There was a guard at the entrance.

"I was told to meet with Nilaon Atticus." He gestured at the elaborately carved wooden doors.

The guard nodded slowly and stepped to the side. Moccasin pushed the door open.

The room was cavernous. It contained

two slit windows that cast long thin beams of light across the sparse furniture and floors. Unusual animal mounts and various ancient-looking weapons lined the walls. A single desk and chair were bleached white with black inlay markings. Another chair of leather sat facing the desk.

Moccasin stood at the entrance waiting to be beckoned forward.

The man sitting in the large, carved chair was as intimidating as the decor. Even seated, it was clear he was a tall nephilim warrior and broad cut as out of stone. He had sharp yellow eyes and dark brown hair. His skin was very pale, and Moccasin noticed the long death-scar running down the side of his neck. Everything about him was authoritative. He wore a leather coat of an unusual burnt-yellow color.

He sat for a moment in silence sizing Moccasin. When finally, he spoke, his voice was deep but jarring to the core. It was a bell toll.

"You are Moccasin. I've been hearing much about you."

There was a pause. Moccasin nodded.

Moccasin eyes landed on a raccoon mount hanging to the left of the door frame. It reminded him of his life on the farm, and he yearned to reach out and touch this one familiar object. "Yes sir." He shut the door, meeting the nilaon's examining gaze.

A small smile slipped across Atticus' lips but didn't reach his eyes. It was a false smile.

He gestured to the seat across from his own. "Please."

Moccasin reciprocated the smile and approached the desk. "You requested to see me?" He asked, settling into a chair

"Yes I did, Moccasin."

He hasn't blinked.

"Is this about my blood tests?"

"It is." Atticus slowly blinked his eyes and folded his arms. He leaned heavily back in his chair. "I'm sure you've been informed about your genealogy. Nephilim and magus."

Moccasin swallowed. "Yes, Sir. Highrindh Jin...insinuated it."

Jin hadn't been lying.

"And you know about our... past experiences with your kind?" The nilaon emphasized these last two words.

My kind?

Where is this going?

A bit of anger began to rise, but he swallowed it.

Atticus spread his hands. "I'm not concerned. I simply want to make sure your loyalty is in the right place." His attempt of seeming genuine came off as arrogance. "For the safety of my people, you see."

"Sir, I can assure you that I mean no harm. Might I ask though...what happen' to make everyone hate magus?"

Atticus shifted in his chair and narrowed

his eyes at Moccasin. "One drove our past nilaon into madness and then suicide."

Moccasin held the nilaon's gaze. "I see."

"Now you understand why I need to assurance of your loyalty. For my soldiers' protection."

"Yes, Sir." Moccasin pushed his glasses up. "You won't have any problems with me." They both understood that Moccasin would be under strict surveillance. It was unspoken that there would be no second chances for any infraction.

Moccasin felt a sudden twinge of regret at the disrespect he had shown Highrindh Jin earlier. He would need to be careful around her.

.....

Chapter Twenty

"**R**emember what I taught you, and you'll be fine. I guarantee it." Bera checked that Moccasin's armor was securely fastened. The armor that he was wearing for the initiation was a standard issue for all recruits. It had rusted patches and was made of heavy fabric and metal. A personalized set was given after initiation was completed.

Moccasin itched his neck under the armor. "Do I have to wear the cotton layer under it?"

Cotton and copper were dangerous for a full magus. He'd learned this from Bera, which explained why he'd felt uncomfortable from the very beginning in his Wakers uniform.

The burning sensation would intensify if he progressed as a magus and strengthened his spells. Moccasin wouldn't learn any magus spells because, as Bera had explained, his magus gene was to be suppressed. He was discouraged from any line of questioning on the subject. It was clear that magus were regarded with suspicion, and their spells were considered dangerous. Bera was unhelpful in how he could learn more about his sensory potential. Despite her resistance, he was able to pull some information reluctantly from her.

There were five basic magus spells. Each required years of practice to master. Touch, smell, taste, sight, and hearing. Some were more difficult than others. Sight and Hearing for instance required extensive training and experience.

Bera tossed him a dagger. "Sorry, cotton is a standard issue." A few more adjustments were made before she decided that everything was to her satisfaction.

She nodded and shook him by the shoulders. "Try not to die. It would be bad for my reputation."

"Oh, I was planning to die right away. Just to shame you." He itched his neck.

"You're next."

"When I die, you can have my glasses." Moccasin chuckled nervously. He ran his fingers along the blade.

"Good luck!" Bera popped her knuckles and rolled her neck. She turned and headed up a flight of stairs to find her seat.

The initiation was an annual spectacle that all of Tavdren anticipated with much enthusiasm. They'd prepared the great hall for the event and planned a day-long celebratory feast. Moccasin heard a muffled scream followed by a cheering crowd.

He watched wide eyed as the door into the great hall was thrown open and one of the Wakers was half carried down the stairs and into chamber for treatment. They seemed to have had the wind knocked out of them.

He was last to go, but he refused to let himself be consumed with fear. Moccasin pushed it down and steadied himself.

The two before him had come away with different types of wounds.

They'd been taken straight back before he could get more than a glimpse.

They must have faced different threats.

Could it be a different initiation for each Nephilim?

Highrindh Dulveron, with his usual fox cape, came down the stairs and gestured to Moccasin. "Come." He said, wiping his hands with a cloth.

Moccasin nodded and ascended the stairs.

.....

When Moccasin took a step into the hall the door slammed behind him, and he could hear the bolt slide into place. To his dismay, the hall was as dark as a moonless night. He could hear sounds and knew that he was being watched by the Tavdren soldiers somewhere around the perimeter. Fighting an unknown opponent in the pitch black wasn't what he had expected, and yet it was all so very Tavdren.

He summoned a small cast. It provided a circle of silver light a few feet in diameter. His glasses slid down his nose. Pushing them up he took careful steps into the void.

This is the moment when something horrible tries to kill me.

The silver cast illuminated his steps as he walked without any direction. Ten feet in and off to his right, something shiny was reflected.

"Hmm. That's somthin'." He cautiously stepped toward it.

Upon closer examination, he discovered they were metal bars. Cell bars. He lifted his hand sending his cast light further. Six cages in total were lined up in a row across the hall.

Moccasin could see spots of blood leading up to and around some of the cages. It was evidence of conflict, although there were no bodies.

Each cage had a plaque with the name of a recruit written upon it. He looked over at the one that remained closed. He knew what the label which dangled from the door would read.

Moccasin Clanon.

A figure was sitting cross-legged in the center. As he drew nearer, he could see it was a petite female. She had cropped dusty, brown hair and the standard prisoner clothes. Her body was covered in dirt and dried blood. He flinched at seeing her lips and eyelids had been stitched closed. They were swollen around the stitching. He found himself unable to look away for the horrific sight.

"Unlock the cage." A smooth voice whispered from inside.

Her mouth couldn't have moved, but the sound was coming from her.

Moccasin took a steadying breath and stepped to the cage door. "They want us to fight?"

"Yes, although I doubt you will kill me." He could hear her thoughts as clearly as if she were speaking. This was a magus spell.

"What makes you think so?" he asked, taking in her poor condition. He could see that her wrists were bound by cotton cords. Red welts were on her arms from where the cotton burned her flesh.

"I never thought I would live to see another nephilim-magus." She said, ignoring his question. "Let me help you, brother. By freeing me, I shall free you. I know how to help you become more." The prisoner held up her hands, showing him her bound wrists. "This is the fate that awaits you. Tavdren will be your destruction."

He challenged her. "You're the magus they've been talkin' about? The one who killed the nilaon?"

"The correct term for a female magus is a hex. You will address me as such."

Moccasin tried to make his cast brighter to get a better look. "They say you killed the past leader."

"Lies." She tried to rise, but alas, the cords of cotton held her down. "They never searched for the murderer, because Atticus accused me! They hate our kind! They fear us! Fear rules them all! Do you think it's a coincidence that the only two nephilim-magus in Tavdren are paired against each other? Atticus is too weak to take me on himself! Release the cotton from my hands! We can both escape! I can show you the secrets of our kind! You don't have to live in their web of magus hate! Spin the web yourself. You'll have more power than them all."

Moccasin was seized with sudden compassion for the poor creature. And a kindled ambition, yet he tried to clear his thoughts and consider the options. There were many, and none were ideal.

Am I considering this?
She's certainly lying.
She could teach me magus spells.

"Once the cotton is removed, I will be able to shape their senses, and we can escape together."

.....

The battle was simple. The Hex had been bound. All he had to do was remove the head from the shoulders. As he approached to attack, knowing her death was upon her, knowing he'd chosen his path, she told him one last thing.

"Lower chamber in the north tower. Hidden in the wall is The Script."

Her death was clean and painless.

Moccasin hadn't taken her advice to flee, but he did take her advice about something else. If he was ever going to survive there, he would need to control the web.

.....

Chapter Twenty-One

Moccasin groomed an appaloosa horse named Beans outside the stables. He whistled peacefully and brushed the horse's mane. Each soldier had a task when they weren't on a patrol or other temporary missions. He had selected work in the barn and stables. It was what he'd been used to on earth. As he worked, he couldn't get the images of the stitched eyelids and lips from the day before out of his mind. That would never happen to him. He wouldn't allow it.

He felt remorse for killing the Hex. Ultimately, it had been beyond his control, but it still left an uneasy feeling in his gut, having killed an innocent. No matter that she'd obviously been using her magus spells on him, twisting his thoughts. No matter that she would've killed him if he'd been persuaded to release her. With all of that in mind, he still couldn't shake her proclaimed innocence of the crime which had her bound for execution.

From his guilty conscience came a thought that the Widow would've been disappointed in him, and it astonished him that his mind would've landed on his mother in regard to this. As if the killing of the hex and the Gwen McClanon were connected.

A small cast came from his fingers. He formed it into the familiar ball shape, then absorbed it back into his fingers. Yawning, he led the horse to its stall and made his way out of the stables. The whistle slowly developed into a tune he remembered from childhood.

Moccasin rubbed his forehead and slowly walked to the barn. He remembered the Hex's final words. He knew of the north tower, although he'd never had an opportunity to go there. He would make time to seek out the script of which she'd spoken. There was no time that day, so if Bera didn't need him, he planned to go the next night.

As if on cue, Highrindh Bera stalked into the barn, and punched him in the shoulder. "You did great! Flawless decapitation!" She praised him with a broad smile.

Moccasin turned on her, "Niloan Atticus needed someone to kill the hex for him."

Bera frowned. "Yes. Of course, he did. You

did your initiation and provided a service to your leader. It looks good for you. Why did you run off so quickly? They are having a celebration feast."

Moccasin shrugged. "Don't feel like it." He rubbed his forehead which was throbbing from the initiation's mental beating. Resisting the hex's magus spells had taken much out of him.

Bera gave him a disappointed look. She sighed and shook her head. "In all my time training you, I still don't understand why you are so solitary."

"Yeah, well I'm not a real nephilim." He whispered to himself.

"Oh, please. You're exaggerating. Besides, you just became a Tavdren soldier. You are one of us, now." She looked him over and sighed. "There's no need for you to be working today. Take some time off."

"Fine."

I will go and get that script.

The two walked silently back to the fort. He didn't want to go to the feast. He didn't want to celebrate a cold victory. The image of the hex's treatment was plastered into his mind.

They did that to her.

What if they plan that for me?

I killed her.

Am I any better?

Bera followed him through the halls to his room. Moccasin cast her a sideways glance. "Do ya have other friends?"

Bera snorted and playfully punched his bicep. He was getting used to her aggressive nature; however, this didn't feel playful but more of an intentional punch. "I have many friends! My brother was here, too! Everyone loved him."

"Brother?" he asked.

Bera's voice was bittersweet at the mention of her brother. "Torald. He was a good man. He had an injury and wasn't a strong caster. That was his downfall." She smiled tenderly.

This uncharacteristic tone from her surprised him. "I'm sorry."

"Yes. Me, also." She turned and quickened her pace away from him. "I'm going to the feast. Hope you feel better."

Moccasin dipped his head respectfully and slipped down the opposite hallway from the noisy celebration in the grand hall.

The headache began to ease.

Thank goodness.

Turning the corner, his arm banged against a door left ajar. His glasses fell off and clinked on the stone floor.

"I have to secure these somehow," Moccasin mumbled and knelt, patting his hands around for them. A shine glistened from under a window. He extended his hand to reach the glasses.

Abruptly a boot stomped next to them. Jin's long pink armored leg startled him. He quickly snatched his glasses off the floor and stood.

"Aren't you goin' to the feast, Highrindh?" Rage bellowed up inside of him, but having learned his lesson the last time, he didn't give her a disrespectful tone.

"I could ask the same thing of you."

Jin's signature pink coat had a new medal on it received from successfully training a recruit. That meant her consultee had also passed their initiation.

"I see your pupil passed their initiation." Moccasin nodded. "Congratulations."

Jin stared, cold and hard. "Cease your chattering." She reached inside her pocket. "Does it need to be said again, that any magus is dangerous for our region?"

Alarm sprang into him at whatever she would pull from her coat. "What have I done? I've passed the invitation. I'm a Tavdren soldier."

"I don't have a problem with you, but I do with the magus kind. Any amount of their blood is dangerous. No matter how much nephilim blood there is to stamp it out."

He prepared himself to make a casting shield.

"What matters is the region's safety, and I won't ever forget what happened to our past nilaon who foolishly trusted that hex." She spat, pulling a piece of cloth out to show him.
It's cotton.

Seeing the fabric, he retreated. "The hex

didn't do it." Moccasin explained to her in a level voice. "We don't have to be enemies. We can be allies."

Jin gripped the cloth. "This is just a warning. Leave Tavdren." With one rapid motion, she gripped his arm and rubbed the caustic cloth into his cheek. Moccasin hissed and kicked her legs out from under her causing Jin to stumbled backward.

Not wanting to get caught in another dispute with Jin, he sprinted toward his chamber. The door was whisked open, and he locked himself inside. His face had angry red welt from the cotton but wasn't badly burned. Because he had yet to do any of the magus spells, his sensitivity wasn't as severe. The pain subsided after he splashed water onto his face, yet as a precaution, he shakily treated the wound to prevent any blisters from forming. The incident had produced more than a red mark, it had left a burning anger.

.....

Chapter Twenty-Two

"What happened to your..." Bera waved her finger at Moccasin's head. "...face. It's uglier than usual."

"You're not nice, ya know that?" Moccasin gently swatted her away her probing fingers.

"I've heard that before," she grinned.

The two were walking into the courtroom. Atticus would be giving a address.

"Ah c'mon." Bera smacked his back. "Tell Aunty Bera what happened."

Moccasin adjusted his shirt. "I accidentally knocked my head with a cast."
Lies!
Oh, shut up.

Bera's face scrunched in confusion. "I

didn't know you could hurt yourself with a cast...only others..." She immediately tried.

His cheek itched around the mild burn. "How long 'til Atticus' speaks?"

"Jin said in five minutes."

The mention of Jin sent a shiver along his spine.

"What's wrong with Jin, anyway?"

Very subtle.

Bera chuckled, opening the door to the court. "Where to begin with that one, aye? Why?"

"She's seemed distracted lately."

Very good.

"Aww, yes." Bera shrugged it off, saying, "Jin has... moods. You'll get used to it." She then left him for her seat in the front next to Jin and Dulveron. The three highrindh spoke together quietly.

The room was full of soldiers talking and laughing. Moccasin found a place beside two younger members. As they eyed him anxiously, one whispered to the other. "That's the Mage."

Ignoring them, he lowered his eyes and began practicing his first magus spell. All magus spells were performed in the mind. They required a mastery of focus. First, there was Smell. That was the easiest to perfect. He knew the incantation, but the noise around him diverted his attention.

His mind ran over the events of yesterday.

At nightfall, while everyone but the perimeter guards were asleep, he'd slipped out of his chambers. Because of the strict curfew, all hallways were clear as he made his way to the lower level. Torches were only lit at intervals, making it easier for him to navigate in the shadows. The highrindh chambers were off the main corridor. His heart had hammered wildly in his chest at the thought of Bera, or worse Jin, discovering him. It was a risk worth taking.

At the entrance to the north tower's lower chambers, he'd discovered four soldiers stationed. They were drunk from the feast and engaged in a tense game of cards. Moccasin surmised that security was minimal, but he needed to get past them to enter the tower.

He approached the card table casually and explained that he was on guard duty upstairs and was bored. So preoccupied with the game were they, that they didn't question his lie. He watched the game while waiting for them to become distracted in the next round of wagers.

As the men became engrossed in the betting, he slipped into the tower and found the door. Using a simple technique that he'd learned from Sampson, it didn't take very long to spring the simple lock. The door came easily open, and Moccasin quietly slid inside and shut it smoothly behind him.

Upon entering, he was overcome with a bracing musty odor. He created a cast to illuminate the pitch-black room, and his eyes slowly adapted to the sight before him. The cast's silver light revealed a storage room lined with shelves which housed hundreds of dusty books and scrolls. Heavy lidded chests lined the far wall and filled the spaces between shelves. Moccasin frowned over the enormity of his task. The hex's script was hidden somewhere in this room.

Well into the night Moccasin searched through each book, scroll, and chests. He moved about and worked silently, so as not to disturb the guards just on the landing. A moment of terror seized him every time a guard passed by on rounds. He waited breathlessly until the clanking footsteps faded up the tower stairwell. Then he could breathe once more. By early morning the dust and musty scent of old paper had filled his lungs causing him to feel nauseous.

Moccasin poured through countless ancient books until his fingers became raw from the cracked leather bindings. He lifted multiple heavy lids from chests and pried open the rusty locks until with the final chest he was still just as empty-handed as when he'd started. Moccasin hadn't come across a single script that was related to magus. Nothing that would've been what the hex had intended for him to find.

Was all this worth it?

There must be something I've overlooked.

Cursing under his breath, Moccasin angrily slid the final chest back into place against the stone wall. The chest made a small impact in the masonry that worried him. His heart stopped beating as he waited to see if anyone would come and investigate the sound. After a few torturous moments, it was clear no one outside had heard.

When he looked behind to examine the damaged chest, he saw the brass hardware had knocked a brick loose in the wall. Moccasin desperately hurried to replace the loosened stone to its original position. There, to his bewilderment, was an opening between two stones. It was more than loose mortar. He raised his cast light to examine it, and found when he pressed his fingers inside, the stone on the left gave way revealing a hidden cubby. Inside the small hole was a single scroll. With unsteady fingers, Moccasin tenderly pulled it from its hiding place. It was thin and extremely delicate. He unrolled the script.

The scroll was aged to the point of being nearly translucent. It was soft and crumbling around the edges from centuries of use. Sitting on stone floor, Moccasin eagerly ran his eyes over the instructions and applications for the five magus spells.

In the silver glow of his cast, Moccasin smiled.

Loud laughter spun him back the present sitting in the courtroom surrounded by soldiers. Looking up, he saw two nephilim quickly glance away. Moccasin glared at them with a single raised eyebrow. Their frightened reactions amused him.

Moccasin had heard enough of the whispering and had seen the sideways stares to understand that word of his nephilim-magus status had made it around the fortress.

"Attention!" Jin barked to the noisy courtroom.

Atticus Coral dipped his head to her. "Thank you, Jin." The nilaon rose from his chair. He wasn't wearing the leather coat which allowed Moccasin to see his armor in full. It was burnt yellow, bright, and dusty grey in spots.

"I want to address you all about a rising conflict between our neighbors."

That can't be good.

Moccasin leaned forward in his chair.

Atticus gestured to the three highrindh. "The four of us have discussed this issue and agreed on how to proceed."

Moccasin thought he saw Jin hide a grimace.

Jin does not agree with the others.

Atticus interrupted the course of thought. "Challavenge, has had disputes with our neighbor, Drundra. They claim Drundra has been violating their borders." Voices bubbled up over the crowded hall.

Jin hissed, and instantly the room returned to silence.

Atticus rubbed his chin. "Drundra is asking us to stand by them in this cause. To do battle, if necessary."

Questions popped up among the soldiers despite Jin's repeated order of silence.

"Are we standing by them?"

"Are the regions at war?"

Realizing he'd nothing to lose, Moccasin called from his seat. "We can't take either side. Our region depends on both for trade." Everyone turned to face him as his voice carried over the chaos. "Involving ourselves in this conflict isn't to our advantage."

The room shuttered to a low hum. Jin was radiating anger at him. "Silence, Mage!"

Atticus put a steadying hand upon Jin's shoulder. "Nonsense. Moccasin has a valid point. I value everyone's input." He turned to face Moccasin. "You are correct. Tavdren won't be taking sides. This was our decision."

The soldiers displayed their agreement by stomping their boots on the stone floor.

It was obvious that Atticus' public and positive acknowledgement of Moccasin enraged Jin. The highrindh had told Moccasin that she had no personal issue with him, but that was a lie. She wasn't hiding it any longer.

.....

"Jin mentioned you in our meeting." Bera checked her nails and looked sideways at him. "Something that would interest you."

"Interest me? What about?"

"She believes you are trying to win Atticus' favor. To gain influence. To promote to a highrindh."

"You know that's not true."

Bera nodded and made a small cast. She played around with it. "I know that, but Atticus doesn't. And... he didn't object to Jin. He might agree-"

"Nah."

"-and after your outburst in hall just now..." She trailed off, knowing what the others would think.

"Bera, it's fine. But if you're really worried, jus' keep an ear out for me."

"I intend to." Bera didn't look pleased.

.....

Chapter Twenty-Three

Moccasin pushed a wheelbarrow of used hay and dumped it behind the barn.

Tending to the livestock in the mornings and evenings was one of his tasks. It reminded him of the McClanon barn. Tavdren soldiers cared for their own horses but the other livestock to the barn was left to the hands. He could see that the stalls, barn, and yard needed many improvements, and he intended to begin the work. The barn had been an integral part of his prior life; it was natural that this was where he'd feel the most at ease.

Everyone worked at the fort. The tasks were scheduled around midday training. The highrindh didn't have a job other than to act as consultants every year to recruits and assisting

Atticus with any regional matters. According to Bera, the latter was time-consuming and not her favorite activity.

He went over his plans for the day.

Finish barn work.

Practice casting.

Practice magus spells.

A spotted black and brown cat dashed past him. Moccasin made a shushing noise and tried to scare it aside. The cat hissed and hid in a bush.

Placing the wheelbarrow handles down, he focused on the cat and tried using the first magus scent spell. He stared at the cat and mumbled the incantation under his breath, thinking through the words carefully. It was a fairly simple spell but draining. He knew he'd achieved his goal when the cat curled its nose and scurried away.

He pumped his fist jubilantly and rolled his sleeves higher up his arms. It had worked. He'd created a displeasing scent to scare the cat. The magus spell made him extremely exhausted, but he was elated to have achieved success.

Maybe one day I can perfect both nephilim and magus skills.

His brief moment of pleasure was abruptly halted. The sound of horses approaching came from up the road, and he turned to see two riders approaching the fortress.

Obeying protocol, Moccasin summoned a

shield-cast. He held the silver shield-cast defensively and positioned himself in the stable road. "State your name and business."

One was wearing the armor of a highrindh. Likey Drundran.

The highrindh sat elegantly upon a large, golden stallion. A short sword was positioned at her side. The other rider appeared to be a Drundran soldier guard.

They reigned in their mounts before Moccasin and the highrindh answered through a shiny navy colored helmet. "I am Chione. I've come to speak with Nilaon Atticus as a representative of Nilaon Hector." The voice was low and female. She spoke slowly and deliberately.

Moccasin removed the shield-cast. "Please, confirm."

The visiting highrindh responded with a curt nod. She dismounted and showed him the back of her hand, upon which was a small blue tattoo. It was her notam.

He remembered Bera showing him a similar tattoo, but red. It was the highrindh brand. Showing allegiance to a region's nilaon.
He nodded respectfully and gestured toward the fort. "Follow me."

When she dismounted, Moccasin found the highrindh to be shockingly small. Although, it was an unfair assessment as he was abnormally tall for a nephilim and all others naturally appeared diminutive. Despite her size, she carried herself with great confidence and pride making her appear much taller.

Highrindh Chione's guard handed their horses reins to a stable hand. Moccasin led the visiting highrindh to the entrance. They walked in silence.

.....

Bera was waiting at the rear entrance with two guards. Evidently, she'd been expecting the arrival of the Drundran delegate. Bera spoke quietly with the soldiers as Moccasin led their guest up the path.

When Moccasin approached his friend, her casual demeanor was gone. Bera's scarred face was cold and tense. She didn't acknowledge him. Instead, she brushed past him and greeted the highrindh.

"Highrindh Chione." She extended her hand.

"You are Highrindh Bera?" Chione took her hand and shook it.

Bera nodded and gestured to her soldiers. "Nilaon Atticus is awaiting you. But first the guards will escort you to your chamber to rest from your journey."

"A guard won't be necessary. I have my own Drundran escort."

"If you wish to enter this building, you will be accompanied by Tavdren guards. It is the procedure."

The two highrindh were in a standoff.

After a tense moment of silent assessing, the visitor consented to be escorted into the fortress.

Bera ordered the guards. "Gashly, please assist Highrindh Chione." As Gashly led Chione through the heavy doors, Moccasin pulled Bera off to the side. "So... what is this all about? What is she talking to Atticus about?"

"This is an official matter and none of your concern."

Moccasin nodded. He looked back to the door. Something in his stomach told him that the highrindh's visit was important.

"What is it, Moccasin?"

"I got a strange feeling from her. That's all."

"She does have that way about her, only because we are from different regions. They say she is soon to become the next leader of Drundra."

This surprised him. "If she's so important then why is she here as a messenger?"

"To send a message, fool." She punched him playfully and cracked her knuckles. "I'm going inside. It's time for breakfast."

"Ah." His glasses began to slip. He pushed them back up. "I still have some work to do. I'll be in shortly."

Bera's boots clanked against the stone steps as she jogged inside.

.....

"Douglas McClanon."

Moccasin winced. Startled at hearing his earth name, he smacked the side of his head against a low beam in the hayloft. Jin's scalding voice could be heard from below in the stable.

Cautiously, he descended the loft ladder and made a shield-shaped cast. "How'd you-"

Jin shrugged and eyed at his silver shield-cast. "All I had to do was look at your waking records. Your history is documented." She tapped a large envelope against her thigh.

"Do what you want with it. I couldn't care less." He absorbed the shield.

Jin shrugged slyly. "Yes, but I might just slip it to Highrindh Chione that you're a magus. She won't take to that very well; I can assure you. Drundra executes magus. Your presence here wouldn't suit her people nor any of our allies. Atticus could be shamed for harboring one of your kind. Do you see the position that your being here puts us all in?"

Moccasin sighed, "What do you want, Jin?"

"Highrindh Jin!" She corrected, holding the envelope tauntingly. "You are going to do exactly what I tell you to do, or your magus genealogy will be slipped out to her or any number of my contacts."

Moccasin snorted. "And what if I tell Atticus of your disloyalty to his leadership? You are threatening to sabotage his inter-regional reputation. Do you think he won't see this as a betrayal? Treason, even?"

"Oh, I think he'll believe whatever I tell him. Do you think he trusts your word over mine? You are, after all, a magus. Shall I remind you of what the last magus did?"

"Just tell me what ya want."

Jin walked over and leaned on a hay bail. "It's pretty simple really. I want you to take all of your magus fooleries and leave Tavdren. The region will be safer without you." Her eyes narrowed. "I would prefer you dead. I could even make that happen; you understand? But if you leave by sunset…well…I'll accept that.

Moccasin attempted to snatch the envelope from her. "I'm not going anywhere."

Jin shook her head and tucked it behind her back. Her lips curled. "You will go. I don't care where to."

She was vicious. Beautiful and treacherous like a panther. Moccasin hadn't trusted her before, but now he understood just how dangerous she could be.

Moccasin took a deep breath and backed away. "I'm not leaving my home. I won't do that again."

"Then I look forward to seeing you in one of those cages. Like the Hex. Stitched and praying for death." The word Hex was spat out angrily. Her teeth gritted together.

He closed his eyes and walked to the stalls. A horse whinnied sensing the building tension.

He had to think of a way out. He wished at this moment he had a magus spell to use. He cursed her.

Jin came up behind him. "You're in no position to argue, Douglas." She clutched the envelope through her pocket. "I will stitch you myself."

Behind him, Moccasin could hear the hum of a cast being created. Spinning swiftly, he met her cast with his own. "Are you crazy?" he deflected the cast and jumped to the side.

"You had your chance, Mage!" Jin shot another cast that grazed his shoulder.

Moccasin grabbed his shoulder in pain as the highrindh hurled another cast, this one aimed at his head.

The following set of events happened with a sensation of being instantaneous and in slow-motion simultaneously. Moccasin moved in a rage that he hadn't known existed. A feeling of self-preservation and aggression welled up through him from a deep, dark place. He spotted the pitchfork he'd been using to haul hay. With a swift motion, he grabbed the pitchfork and stabbed it into Jin. The highrindh froze in complete shock, her bulging eyes locked onto him in disbelief and wonder. As Moccasin pulled the prongs slowly out of her body, he watched in terror as she fell limp to her knees, clutching her middle. Blood seeped through her fingers and onto the stable ground. Moccasin backed away, not having any idea what to do next. Her lifeless body lay staring up at him.

.....

Chapter Twenty-Four

Moccasin's eyes widened with panic as he repeatedly played over the events in his mind.

It had happened so fast.

She wouldn't stop.

And the pitchfork was there.

I had no choice.

I could have just left!

Jin's lifeless eyes stared up at him. The blades of the pitchfork had penetrated her chest. Blood dribbled down through her clothing and puddled around her torso, staining the hay-strewn ground. The bright pink in her eyes had faded, turning to grey. Her casting energy had left her body, leaving only a shell.

Moccasin took a long and steadying

breath.

She is gone.

After several furious minutes of pacing, he decided to hide the body. They'd never believe she had attacked him. Not even Bera. Jin was a highrindh and he was a magus, after all. And he knew he wouldn't stand any chance of running. They'd come after him and eventually track him down. Disposing of the weapon and her body where they would never be found was his only recourse.

Moccasin could hear Widow McClanon in his mind. *"Lyin' is a dead end."*

This was not earth. This was Tavdren, and he had to do what was necessary to survive.

.....

Moccasin collapsed on his bed. All evidence and traces of Highrindh Jin had been disposed of so meticulously that no one would ever be able to place her in the barn. His shoulders ached from the labor. God willing, no one would suspect him.

Jin had many allies. The search for her would be ongoing for a long time.

He'd buried Jin deep in the birch forest beside a boulder with the stream running nearby. This had all been done in the bright sunlight of midmorning, with voices in the distance and birds flying between tree branches overhead. He didn't dare risk waiting until nightfall. The body would've been discovered.

A few nephilim had passed by him, however they didn't think much of the wheelbarrow full of hay being pushed by a stable hand. Moccasin had thought that they surely would see his sweat and hear the thudding heart in his chest. They must've seen some part of the body hiding under the hay. It wasn't until they each walked on out of sight, that he could continue his task.

The smell and images were burned into his brain.

A knock sounded at his door, bringing him out of the horrific memory. The sound was amplified in his paranoia and jarred him. He leaped up and hurried to the door. "Yeah?"

"Moccasin?"

"Hello, Bera. How are you?" He leaned against the door, self-conscious of his hands. His forced smile. His worried brow.

"You didn't show up for breakfast...or lunch. Is something wrong?" She tilted her head. "You seem...."

He scratched his neck. "A couple of the horses got loose."

"Ah..." She narrowed her eyes. "Have you seen Jin? Atticus wants the highrindh to meet to discuss his meeting with Highrindh Chione."

"No." He scratched more. "Sorry." He searched her face for any sign of suspicion, but Bera's expression was completely neutral. Moccasin shrugged while forcing a yawn. "I'm sorry, I can't help you. Maybe ask one of her friends?

Does she have any?"

Bera smiled. "Alright, then. Sorry for bothering you."

Am I imagining it, or is Bera acting stranger than I am?

.....

Atticus sat in his chair and addressed the chamber with a melancholy tone. The dark circles under his eyes emphasized his lack of sleep. "As you've heard. Highrindh Jin is gone." Although they had disagreed on certain matters, the two had been close confidants, and it was clear he was taking the loss of Jin hard.

Moccasin sat toward the back. Like Atticus, he also had lost sleep due to the recent events. He'd distracted himself from his dire situation by taking up his magus training with renewed vigor. For the last week, he'd made progress on scent, taste, and touch spells. Hearing and sight were far too complicated to attempt.

The other two highrindh, Bera and Dulveron were seated by Chione, who'd remained at the fort. Rumors had circulated that she was trying to convince Atticus that Tavdren should join Drundra in their conflict with Challavenge.

Atticus silenced the murmuring crowd. "I haven't decided on my third highrindh, but I will be taking the recommendations of the other two." He paused briefly. "If anyone has information on Jin's whereabouts, you must come forward. The search will continue."

What mystified Moccasin was how Atticus didn't know Jin was dead. When she'd died, the highrindh brand, or notam, would've faded from her hand. There were ways to remove the brand, but that would be considered treason. Either way, he would certainly know as his matching brand would also fade.

Why is Atticus pretending he believes the mysterious note?

The only possible explanation was that Atticus, and his highrindh, were setting a trap. Was this all a plot to draw him out? How much did Bera know?

After the meeting was dispatched, Moccasin tried to catch up to Bera. Before he managed to reach her in the crowded hall, Atticus took his two remaining highrindh into his study.

Moccasin spotted Chione standing at the small window, absently making a small cast. It was unusual to see her without armor. Her hair was dark navy. She had bright blue eyes and wore unusual decorative blue paint on her cheeks and nose. Chione was clearly a strong casting nephilim.

Catching him watching her, she stepped off the dais and left the hall.

There would be time to speak with Bera tomorrow.

.....

Chapter Twenty-Five

Moccasin made his way to Atticus' office with much trepidation. The leader had requested to speak with him. A week marked by anxiety and fear had gone by without anyone connecting him to Jin's disappearance. While searching Jin's suite for information, Highrindh Bera had found a note stating Jin was leaving. There were personal reasons given in the letter, but none were revealed to the soldiers. Rumors spread, yet nothing was confirmed. This caused great concern in his mind and raised many questions.

Who wrote the note?

Is this part of a trap?

The guard opened the doors upon Moccasin's arrival but didn't announce him. Moccasin adjusted his glasses and entered. He heard voices from around the corner where Atticus' desk was situated. He recognized the voices.

Atticus was having a heated debate with the Drundran Highrindh Chione.

"If Tavdren won't join us in this, Challavenge will come after Tavdren next. This war is coming to you whether you like it or not."

"I won't risk the lives of my region over your border dispute."

"It's more than a border dispute! They are expanding into our region! It is an invasion."

Moccasin tried to back out of the office, yet his movement revealed his presence to Atticus.

"Moccasin! Come in." He looked at Chione. "Our conversation is over."

Moccasin tried to avoid eye contact with the highrindh.

Chione's eyes narrowed as she looked over to Moccasin.

Atticus spoke to Chione. "Now, I assume your business here is done? You came to present your case, and I have given my answer." He held his hand out. "I will send you with an escort."

"This is unnecessary." Chione shook the nilaon's hand as a formality before leaving. She glanced sideways at Moccasin and exited the office.

Moccasin exhaled and turned to Atticus with a last attempt to get out of the meeting. "If now is a bad time. I can return...."

"No." Atticus stared up at the ceiling. "I want to speak with you about Jin's disappearance."

Moccasin swallowed. "Yes, Sir."

"I need your assistance."

"I'm not sure how I could help you."

Does he know?

Atticus made himself comfortable in his chair. "I have reasons to believe that Jin didn't flee." He paused. "I believe she was killed."

Was Atticus watching him too closely? A storm swelled up inside him at hearing those words, and it took everything in his power to keep it from showing itself. "Why do you think that?"

"Not important." The leader made an unreadable face and leaned in. "What's important, is that the killer might be one of my own soldiers."

"Really?" Moccasin's heartbeat surged. His eardrums throbbed.

Breath, fool.

"Yes. This is why I need your help." Atticus gestured to Moccasin. "I believe we could use your...special skills...to help find the killer. We will bring in our suspects, and you could..." He struggled to find the right words. "make them think you have magus spells."

Moccasin's panic calmed.

He doesn't know.

"You mean interrogation? You want me to

interrogate our soldiers?"

"Correct." Atticus continued, "You see. Not everyone knows the script was destroyed. Most still believe it exists, and you can make our suspects believe you have it, no?"

"I'm not sure..."

Atticus made a thin smile. "You'd be providing a great service to your region. Besides, finding her killer could help you earn others' trust."

"Sir-"

"This isn't a request."

.....

Chapter Twenty-Six

The next night Moccasin was laying in his bed trying to sleep. The memory of Jin's final moments still haunted his thoughts, and now he was playing a dangerous game with his fellow soldiers. Paying a losing game with Bera and Atticus, as well. The deceit was so interwoven now, it was a challenge to keep his lies straight. This was the web.

Staring at the shadows along a wall of his room, Moccasin's eyes began to blink heavily on the verge of sleep when a faint mist began to gather in the corner. As his mind slowly processed what he was seeing, the mist swirled into a form. The figure in white took shape and came forward out of the mist. With his recent troubles, he'd forgotten about the white vision. It seemed like a dream from long ago. A dream long forgotten. But there she was, in her horrifying beauty, clothed all in white. The phantom, for that is what he still believed her to be, was now staring at him from the foot of his bed. Her movement took Moccasin by surprise, and he jumped from his bed, conjuring a defensive cast.

The two stared at each other for an uncomfortable amount of time. Finally, with his heart hammering against his ribs, Moccasin broke the silence and whispered. "Who are you?"

For a brief moment, the figure looked as if she was going to respond, instead a faint smile grew across her face.

"Are you a ghost? Or something worse?"

The lady nodded slowly.

"You understand me?"

She nodded again.

"Can you speak?"

Another nod.

Moccasin began to wonder if he was dreaming.

"Are you here to kill me?"

She shook her head.

"What do you want from me? Do you need help?"

The figure shook her head. *"I'm here to help myself."*

Moccasin's eyes widened. He didn't expect her voice to sound lifelike. It was a slow and quiet voice.

"You can speak?"

"When I wish." The ghostly woman gave him another unsettling smile. *"I chose my host wisely."*

"Host?"

"My selected decedent. It was either you, or the other." She replied. *"You were the right one. Yes."*

What is she talking about?

What does she mean by Host?

"Are you the ghost of a nephilim?"

"No. I am a keeper."

Moccasin felt his eyes widen. "Your one of the five keepers?"

The lady in white snarled and disappeared through a wall. *"Six! There were six keepers! My five brethren cut me out! They killed me. And in doing so, killed themselves."* He could hear her voice from wherever she had gone.

"What do you need from me?" He asked, spinning around expecting her to reappear in the now empty room.

"My keeper brethren and I have physically died, so a host in this realm is required. We must live through one of our kin." Abruptly the lady re-appeared, standing before him, jolting him back in terror.

"I don't understand."

The Keeper nodded. *"We borrow your physical bodies to return to our home realm. Aurum, The Golden Realm. The Creator cursed us here."* Her beautiful and terrifying face was framed by white hair that loosely flowed about her shoulders when she moved. Where eyes would have been were now only empty sockets that gleamed maroon.

"That means you...have been inside...." Moccasin drew in his cast and put his hand upon his chest.

"Indeed. Fear not, I have no intentions of harming you, unless you become difficult. In some hundred years, two more keepers will arrive in this afterlife. You'll find it in both of our interests to dispose of one."

"You want me to kill a keeper for you?"

"For us, child."

She moved over to the slit window. He could see through her form in the moonlight. Her gown was a mist in the pale light.

"Two keepers are already here, one of which, you've already befriended. The keeper who shares her body is not a threat. He is foolish and pleasures himself on appearance and whims."

She turned back to face him. *"My enemy will arrive, and when he does, you are going to destroy him by killing his host. He will be your enemy as well, make no mistake. Our fates are sealed together."* The ghost keeper began to fade from his vision.

Moccasin blinked in the darkness trying to determine that she was indeed gone. He stood there for several moments, trying to recall everything she'd said.

I'm not going to help her.
I'm not going to get in between these keeper's affairs.

For safe measure, he checked the door lock and jumped into his bed and childishly pulled the covers up over his head. Everything he'd just been told made no sense to him.

Moccasin willfully chose to ignore it and decided it was better left as a dream.

.....

Chapter Twenty-Seven

He once again found himself at the top of the grassy hill, overlooking the Tavdren fortress. He was watching the flames consume the roof structure from inside and the surrounding forest. He saw the stables and barns burning. Everything was blurry.

"Watch it burn." A low voice hissed next to him. The voice was familiar.

He turned to whom the voice belonged. Beside him was the white vision. He now knew it was the keeper inside him. He tried to get a hold of her, but he was fixed in place. His actions weren't under his control. His emotions were as blurry as the keeper.

"I don't boast." His voice sounded older and harsh to his ears.

He knew that he was in the dream again.

He couldn't wake from the horrific scene he believed to be from his own mind. Only it didn't feel like a dream anymore. It felt like a warning. A portent of what was to come.

.....

Part Three

.....

Chapter Twenty-Eight

Over one hundred years had passed in the Nephilim Realm. Moccasin inspected a line of soldiers in uniform. "Your blade needs sharpening." He switched the soldier's sword out and sent the dull blade to the armory with a page. "Don't come to me with it like that again. You won't get a second chance."

"Yes, Sir."

Twenty years ago, after the death of Dulveron, Moccasin took place as a highrindh. Highrindh Bera and Highrindh Grace, who'd been his consultee, were his peers.

"Be thankful I caught it before Atticus." His Georgian accent had faded. It was now only slightly noticeable.

Bera was returning from the Waking Center with the recruits.

This group should be big.
Some have been asleep for ten years now.

For an undisclosed reason, the physicians at the Waking Center decided to Awaken every decade, not annually. Moccasin didn't care to question why.

Apart from his faded accent, some new scars were visible, along with the high-rindh notam. Moccasin didn't appreciate Atticus knowing his every location, but it was something with which he'd to live. The tracker only worked while both nilaon and highrindh were alive, which is why they'd never found Jin's body.

The soldiers were approved and sent off to form their patrols. Atticus' heavy armored boots rang on the stone. "How do they look?"

"Good. We should be in decent shape for the new group of Wakers." He stretched. "When will they arrive?"

"This afternoon. Is everyone informed?"

"Yes. Everyone's been informed of the meeting for their arrival." Moccasin pushed his glasses into a better position. "Has Bera radioed?" Since his waking, Nephilim technology had greatly improved. They were still behind earthly technology, but having radios made life convenient. For older nephilim, these advancements were giant leaps, but for recent Wakers, the afterlife could feel like a great step back in time.

Atticus sighed and shook his head. "You

two shouldn't be so dependent on your friendship. There might come a time when you find yourselves to be enemies."

Moccasin glanced over to his leader. "We'll cross that bridge when we come to it."

Atticus patted the nephilim-magus on the back before he walked to the courtroom, leaving Moccasin alone with the remembrance of his own Waking.

That was so long ago.

.....

Moccasin spoke with Grace on the dais. She was the first highrindh in Tavdren history to be promoted in less than a hundred years after waking. Her complex military strategies and valiant presence among the lower ranks were to thank for her success. Grace was quiet and efficient.

She'd been Moccasin's chosen pupil before being promoted to highrindh.

The great hall doors opened, and Bera entered with seventeen Wakers. Fatigue and confusion marked their faces. They were fresh from their journey and ill-prepared for the life ahead. With every new group, he remembered what he'd felt walking in this room. Like these, Bera had been his guide.

She came forward to join the other highrindh on the raised platform. Moccasin greeted her warmly. Bera's long red hair was pulled tightly back in a braid. Her eyes were darkened and tired, but she didn't let it show in her demeanor.

Following on Bera's heels, was Vali, a massive grey wolf with a white underbelly and yellow eyes. The wolf had been her constant companion for many years.

Moccasin recalled the day when he'd been introduced to Vali. It was very odd like most things involving Bera. He'd been searching for her one afternoon to inquire about numbers of horses that would be needed for evening grounds patrol.

"Bera?" he had asked on entering her rooms. "Which..." His eyes then landed on the creature that had been sitting on its haunches behind her chair. Startled, he whispered, "Don't move."

Bera glanced up from her work. "What? What do you need?"

"Just...don't...don't turn around."

Bera then immediately looked over her shoulder. "What? Vali?"

"There is a wolf, Bera." he recalled gesturing, "Right there."

"Yes. It is a wolf." Bera spun in her chair and scratched Vali behind her large ears. "I call her, Vali."

"I can see it's a wolf! What is it doing in here?"

"Probably looking for her supper."

"How long have you had that in the fort?"

He had asked in utter disbelief.

"That is rude. She could ask the same of you." Bera stroked Vali's head. "And if you must know, since last night. We met while I was hunting."

"You have a pet wolf?" Moccasin had sighed and rubbed his forehead. "Of course, you do."

"Well, no." Bera had looked back at Vali, affectionately. "She is here of her own free will. Vali is no pet. She can come and go as she pleases."

Somehow, Moccasin didn't remember being surprised. Having a wolf was the most Bera thing for Bera to do. And by now he was used to the great beast and smiled at the memory as the two took their places on the dais.

Vali settled at her feet as Bera found her seat beside him. "What did I miss?" She asked with more energy than the newest of Wakers.

He rubbed his stubbled chin. "Not much. Patrol caught a village thief breaking into the storehouse. Besides that, nothing."

Bera slapped her hands on her knees. "Ha! I find that hard to believe. Usually, everyday has some crisis. Guess I took it with me."

"Or maybe it is just you who starts all the problems."

Bera punched his shoulder.

The humorous moment was halted by Atticus' entrance. The room fell silent.

Moccasin was suddenly reminded of the white vision. The keeper hadn't returned since her last visit after Jin's death all those years ago, but he'd thought of her frequently. What she'd claimed appeared to be true. There were records of a sixth keeperial being, but no one knew the name. Only that a sixth keeper might have existed.

Atticus began his speech. "Welcome, new Wakers. By now you have received basic information about Tavdren. Anything else you need to know will be taught to you by a mentor, or consultant. Each of you will be assigned one. The highrindh, our generals, will choose first." He gestured to Bera. "Highrindh Bera."

"Thank you, Nilaon Atticus." Bera stood and wandered to the edge of the stage. She looked down at the Wakers.

As highrindh who'd been the guide, it was Bera who'd get the first pick. Because she had spent time with this group, her pick would probably be the one with the most power. She always chose well.

She selected a Waker with fair skin, bright green eyes, and dark brown hair.

The man looked very familiar. The pale skin, the cut of the jaw and mouth made Moccasin's mind race. The man looked uncannily like Atticus.

Could they be related?

Children were born in Hazdrim, however

raising children in Tavdren's wasn't wise in his opinion, and it was expressly forbidden for Nilaon and Highrindh. Any soldier within the fortress wishing to start a family was required to leave.

How could they be related?

If this man is indeed Atticus' relation, Bera will have a hard time training him.

Will Atticus claim him as kin?

If he does acknowledge the man, will he take control of the training?

Moccasin looked over to Atticus and tried to ascertain any sort of reaction, but there was none. The leader nodded and looked to Grace.

Grace selected her Waker quickly.

"Highrindh Moccasin." Atticus motioned for him to rise.

The Waker that caught his attention was a tall young man with black skin and a kind face that reminded him of Sampson. His casting color was probably purple, due to the man's striking violet eyes. He appeared eager and good-natured. A willing student was a good sign.

"You." He pointed to the Waker and returned to his seat next to Bera. Moccasin couldn't be sure, but as he turned, he thought he saw the young man give him a thumbs up and a wink.

The rest of the Wakers were promptly selected by soldiers in order of seniority and shown to their chambers. Moccasin and Bera spilled a bit of gossip as they headed to their suites. They would meet with their consultees in the courtyard the following morning.

·····

Moccasin slept in a tangle of covers. The night before, he'd imbibed unwisely and the loud banging noise at his door jarred him awake, clutching his throbbing forehead. He rolled off the bed and hopped into training pants.

The knocking increased in volume.

"I'm coming!" he growled, pulling at a boot.

Someone's going to lose a finger for this.

He grumbled and tripped over to the door.

"Bera, I swear to-" Moccasin swing the door opened but was stunned to see his new consultee. Not Bera. "What the-" He growled, brushing a hand over his stubbled jaw.

"Good morning, Sir!" The Waker smiled in greeting and extended a mug in his hand. "I brought you coffee."

"Son. What the hell are you doing waking me up this early?" Moccasin snarled, grabbing the coffee. "You were supposed to wait in the courtyard."

The young man flinched. "I'm sorry, Sir. I'm just excited and thought we could get our groove on."

"Groove, what?" Moccasin's eyes narrowed, sipping coffee. "How did...who told you where to find my room?"

"The red highrindh, Sir."

Moccasin ran his fingers through his unwashed hair and grumbled, "I'll speak with her later. For you, right now. Turn and leave."

"Sir?"

"Get." Moccasin sighed. "Training begins in an hour."

.....

Moccasin found the young Waker in the courtyard, and as he approached, he looked the Waker up and down. "What's your name, kid?"

"Benjamin, but my friends call me Benji, Ben, Owl, B-" He held out a finger for each nickname.

Moccasin blinked. "Yeah?" He sighed and rubbed his stiff neck. "Well, I'm just gonna call you Ben, okay?"

"Okay! What about you? What do I call you?"

"Highrindh Moccasin."

Ben tilted his head. "Hmm. You don't seem like a Moccasin." His brow furrowed, then he brightened. "Can I call you Snake? That's cool." Ben pointed his finger at Moccasin.

Like lightning, Moccasin grabbed hold of Ben's finger and gritted between his teeth. "Only if you want your finger broken."

Using Ben's finger as leverage, Moccasin pushed him down the pathway. "Let's start with the basics. You've been told about nephilim casting?"

Twisting up and walking on his toes to

avoid pain, Ben stammered, "Ya...yeah! Miss Bera showed us how on the way here! I can show you!"

"Miss Bera." Moccasin snorted and let go of his finger. "Show me, then."

Ben shook out his finger and took a deep breath to steady his nerves. In short order, he began forming a tiny purple cast. It was a wispy dagger and was impressive for a Waker, though Moccasin was too tired and hungover to admit it.

"Needs work."

They'd arrived in the empty training field where Moccasin had been trained and where he had trained countless other recruits, including Highrandh Grace.

Moccasin turned to face his new consultee. "Make it into a shield."

"That seems pretty difficult, Sir. I've only learned this one." Ben absorbed the purple cast.

"In battle, a shield-cast can save your life. You'll have to be able to make one in seconds." Moccasin made one to prove his point. The shield-cast was so compact that it appeared to be solid gleaming silver.

Ben gawked at the shield in awe. The simple cast greatly impressed him. "Get out, Man! That's beautiful! It looks like a disco ball!"

"A what?" Moccasin had experience with Wakers from periods following his death, but current twentieth-century Wakers were particularly bizarre.

Ben replied. "A ball of light for dancing."

"There is no dancing here!" Moccasin grabbed Ben's collar and pulled him forward to stare in his face. "Got it?"

"Sure thing!" Ben held his thumbs up. "So, I just picture the shape...right?"

"Yes. Focus on your shape. Make a clear image in your mind of what your cast will become."

"I'll try." Ben froze and concentrated on his hands. A small blotchy shield projected. Moccasin nodded and pulled his cast back, leaving the space between them glowing with faint purple lighting.

"That's a good start. Keep practicing. Practice is the only way to perfect a cast."

"Groovy!"

.....

Chapter Twenty-Nine

Voices coming from up the path alerted Moccasin and Ben that two nephilim were coming to the field. They stopped training and waited to see who was approaching. A great furry beast could be seen bounding ahead. No other nephilim had a wolf escort.

"Moccasin, mind if we train with you?" Bera jogged over and bumped into his shoulder.

Vali sat panting next to Bera's chosen consultee as if in a guard position. The Waker curled his nose at Vali's proximity. The large wolf had visibly unnerved him. Vali had that effect on people.

"Sure."

"You look terrible! Rough night?"

Moccasin glared at Bera and nodded in Ben's direction, "Not as rough as this morning."

"Ah, you got my wake-up call!" Bera laughed, "You're welcome! Nice Waker you got there. Has he told you about roller skates and roller rinks? He told me all about it."

Moccasin frowned. He held his hand out to the Atticus look-alike. "And you? What's your name?"

The man answered in a heavy Russian accent. "Wift T. Stillwood is my chosen Nephilim name."

Moccasin nodded. "Welcome to hell."

Ben attempted another shield cast, but it was still translucent and weak. Bera instructed Wift to join him in the practice. His casting color was vibrant green.

Moccasin pulled Bera to the side. "What's this guy's story?"

Bera looked confused. "What do you mean?"

"Oh, come on!" He put his hands in his pockets and watched Bera closely for some sign. Some clue. "Doesn't Wift remind you of anyone?"

Bera chuckled. "No. Why, does he to you?" She turned over her shoulder and squinted at Wift.

Moccasin narrowed his eyes and grunted, "Bera. He's the very image of Atticus."

"Don't see it." She averted his questioning gaze. It was clear she was lying.

"You don't see it?" He sighed. "Bera!"

"Okay, fine!" She whispered sharply. "I

thought I could impress Atticus. You know. By training his son."

Son?

He groaned and stared her dead in the eyes. She was lying once again. "Bera?"

"What?"

Moccasin frowned, scrutinizing her expression. "That might be the dumbest excuse, I've heard. What are you up to?"

"I know what I'm doing, alright." Bera hissed, "And you're no one to talk...dumb excuse."

She wasn't herself. His gut told him that Bera was keeping something from him. He knew her well enough, but he wouldn't be able to pressure her into revealing it. He was patient. After all, he'd kept Jin's death a secret for over a hundred years. There was a lot of time in Hazdrim.

"Hey, Mr. Moccasin!" Ben rushed over. He had executed a fully casted purple shield. "I did it!"

"Highrindh Moccasin." he corrected. "Good job, Benjamin."

"I thought you were calling me Ben?"

"Does it matter what I call you?"

Ben looked perplexed at this but realizing that his consultant was not in a good mood, he let it go.

Wift tried to copy the shield cast. His also appeared as a solid shape. Bera and Ben were very excited by it. Moccasin noticed that they both shared a high level of enthusiasm. He didn't give Wift any praise. Wift was not his trainee, and Moccasin enjoyed that his indifference visibly irritated Bera.

"Ben, we're finished for today. See the steward about your tasks. He will give you an assignment and instructions," Moccasin explained and turned to leave before any further questions.

Walking past, he saw Wift attempting a different cast.

He hasn't spoken a single word but his name.

Bera patted his back. "Get some rest, Moccasin."

.....

Moccasin went to Atticus' office. Maybe it was curiosity, or maybe it was the whiskey. Either way, he was determined to figure out if Wift was Atticus' son, as Bera had claimed. Because of his highrindh rank, the guard at the door let him pass. Moccasin knocked on the wooden door.

Some remote part of his brain knew this was a bad idea. A very small part. But it was too late to change his mind, however, when Atticus beckoned him.

"Moccasin. What do you need?"

"I'd like to speak with you."

"I have some time." Atticus gestured to the chairs at his desk.

Moccasin nodded and took a seat. Atticus sat across from him. "Is something wrong with your consultee?"

"No. Ben is doing well. He has talent." He removed his glasses and cleaned them with his shirttail. He was on his sixteenth pair. Bera had been right, she'd broken the first pair and many after.

Where to start, huh?

He put them back on and said, "It's something Bera said about her trainee."

Atticus frowned and the lines between his eyes deepened. "What all did she say?"

He is worried.

Moccasin drummed his fingers on his thigh. "Wift seems to be...talented. He has natural ability. What's bizarre is that he...well, I have noticed that he looks a lot like-"

Atticus raised his palms.

"-You."

The two men stared at each other until the nilaon broke the silence. "We won't discuss Stillwood any further." He whispered, his voice thick and strained. He rose and pointed to the door. "Unless you have something else to discuss, you may leave."

"I apologize." Moccasin nodded, his mind swarming with Atticus' admission by default. He rose to leave.

Atticus' refusal to answer the question gave Moccasin all the information he needed. That was as far as he would go. Asking again might lead to consequences.

I'll do some investigating on my own.

I need to go about this a different way.

.....

"How is this?" Ben asked.

"Try casting different objects as fast as you can. Shield, sword, axe, and spear." Moccasin instructed Ben. "Let's see it."

Ben nodded. He shut his eyes and made a shield-cast. The shield turned into a sword. Then an axe. And finally, a spear.

"Your forms are solid. Try faster. Cast speed is an advantage." Moccasin stood next to him with his arms crossed and his feet planted shoulder-width apart. "Have you been practicing during your free time?"

"Yes, Sir!"

"The initiation is tonight."

Ben reabsorbed the cast. His violet eyes were glazed with confusion. "What happens during the initiation?"

Moccasin remembered his own initiation with the hex. It was a painful memory. He now knew that the hex had been using a spell on him. That she'd not been completely defenseless. Over time he'd even convinced himself that her death had been noble, though he knew it was not. "I can't say. It's somethin' everyone has to experience, and it's a little different for everyone. You'll do fine."

"Can I ask something?" Ben grabbed his water flask from a bench and drank a few sips.

"Yes."

He'd better not ask for a hug.
He's going to ask for a hug.

Ben put his water down and sat on the bench. "I was talking with Wift and Afin. They say you're a magus?"

This wasn't what he had expected, and he was thrown off. "And?"

"So..." Ben drank another sip. "...what is it? What's a magus?"

"Nephilim-magus are a nephilim breed with abilities to manipulate senses with spells. We can manipulate smell, touch, taste, hearing, and sight." Moccasin explained. Being a magus was a topic he had to cover with all of his trainees, eventually. "The Script has been destroyed, so it's of no importance."

Ben was confused. "I thought only nephilim could be in this realm?"

"Yes. I am part keeper and part magus. I am both. The keeper blood makes me a nephilim while the magus blood makes me a mage. I am not a full mage. All magus here are nephilim-magus."

Ben nodded and slouched. "How many magus are in Hazdrim?"

"I'm the only one in Tavdren. Apparently, Golovarn has a very large magus population. But I'm not certain of their numbers." Moccasin frowned.

Ben regretted bringing up the subject. "I'm sorry for asking."

Moccasin loudly clapped his hands to get Ben's mind in place. "Back to business. Have you been practicing the drills I assigned?"

"Of course! Want to see?"

"I thought that was implied?"

Ben planted his feet and went through all the drills without mistake.

He should make it through the initiation.

Each prisoner was selected purposely for the individual Waker to create the best challenge for the consultee and the audience.

Moccasin knew the prisoner they'd assigned to Ben. The consultant had to assure the prisoner would be a good challenge. No one wanted a boring fight. His own initiation was the exception. Atticus had been adamant that the hex should be bound.

"Do you think I'll pass my initiation?" Ben asked excitedly.

"You will. I only train the best of the lot. Why waste my time with someone who could fail? You're a reflection of me when you are in there. Remember that!"

"I'm not the best."

"You don't think so? Well, then all you have to do is not be the worst." Moccasin thumped Ben's head.

"Ow!"

"Always motivate yourself. Never doubt your ability. Doubt is your enemy. A negative attitude will only bring failure." He thumped him again.

"Ow! Yes, Sir."

"Go get in your uniform. You'll perform better if you're comfortable in the armor."

"Right on!"

I don't know what that means.

Ben hurried to get changed, leaving Moccasin alone in the training hall.

.....

Chapter Thirty

Moccasin sat with Bera and the other consultants. The viewing gallery overlooked the main hall from above on all sides. The entire chamber was completely dark until each combatant entered and created their first cast. The cast would illuminate the fighting below in an eerie glow. Tavdren enjoyed the gladiator-style scene, but Moccasin was indifferent. He only cared that his consultee fought well, and only because it was a reflection on him.

The prisoners were carefully selected from those condemned to death by the group of consultants and Atticus. The purpose of the battle was to test the recruits' battle preparedness. *Can they kill?*

It was necessary to know this before going to war. The prisoner would be led to the darkened hall and left to fend for themselves with whatever casts they could conjure. On the rare occasion the prisoner won the battle, they would have earned their freedom. The victorious would be banished forever from Tavdren, but alive and free.

That is what the hex had wanted. Freedom. But he knew Atticus well enough now to know that he wouldn't have honored that pledge if Moccasin had been careless and allowed the hex to defeat him. The hex was the only combatant to have ever been bound. Her deadliest weapon had not been the kind that required hands. She had very nearly convinced him to release her.

Wift was fighting his prisoner. The Waker made a long sword-cast, and instantly jammed it into the prisoner's chest. The prisoner fell to the ground while in the process of shield-casting. It was a very efficient kill. Bera beamed with pride, as she had successfully trained another capable soldier.

"Well done, Bera." Moccasin congratulated her with a side hug.

"Thank you! He might be the best trainee I've ever had."

Moccasin clicked his tongue against the roof of his mouth. "Really?"

Bera rolled her eyes and punched him. "Most definitely."

The guards led Wift out of the arena.

Moccasin watched impassively as the body was dragged out. Blood was dried up with cloths to allow for the next round.

Ben was the last of the recruits to be tested. They'd all passed, some with more injuries than others. He watched Ben make a shield-cast upon entering. The Waker cautiously walked to the center ring where his opponent's cage had been set. Everyone whispered and placed bets on how the combat outcome.

Moccasin held his breath as Ben approached the cage and spoke a few indecipherable words with the prisoner. The cage was opened. Moccasin exhaled as the battle began.

It took longer than it should've. Ben was slow in his advances. He appeared reluctant to engage, and that concerned Moccasin. He was leaving himself open and giving his opponent time to cast offensively. Ben would surely die if he didn't have the survival instinct of a combat warrior. These initiations were about finding out who did and who did not.

Bera turned to Moccasin and he could feel her smug grin in the darkness.

After what felt like hours, Ben proved himself capable. The prisoner had instigated the majority of the combat, which made Ben's casts primarily defensive. He wasn't able to turn to the offensive position until the death blow. It was a lucky opening, and they all knew it. Once again, that gravely worried Moccasin. Ben would be highly criticized, and that criticism would lead back to him.

"Man, he really screwed up." Bera slapped him on the back, chuckling.

"Thanks, Bera. How kind of you to point it out."

"Well, yes. Skates showed compassion. That's a valuable...trait...in some circumstances."

"Compassion isn't rewarded here," He mumbled, placing his hands over his mouth and running them up to his forehead and through his hair. "I'm going to beat the lights out of that disco-headed numbskull."

Over her shoulder and from all sides, Bera collected her winnings. "Moccasin. You're over-reacting." She slipped the foalds into the pocket of her brown leather jacket.

Moccasin was incredulous. "You bet against Ben?"

"No, I bet against your judgment." She shrugged. "You picked poorly this time. Skates has a kind soul." Skates was her new nickname for Ben. Moccasin could not counter that. It was the truth, and he knew it.

"Just come to the initiation party. You'll forget all about it."

"You know I don't like these parties. Nothing ever goes right during them."

"Nope." She got up and crossed her arms. "You're coming. Some fun might help get that stick out of your butt, besides I need a drinking buddy."

She waved some of her winnings, and smiled, "It's on me! Or rather, it's on you and Ben!"

His mouth fell open. "Wow. That's low."

Bera ignored his comment and pushed him towards the exit.

.....

The party was little more than a lively dinner party. In the past, the moment Atticus left, the festivities would ratchet up. The Nephilim would go to their cups hard, and the laughter, music, and arguments would grow as the night progressed. Tonight, would be no exception, but at that moment everyone was minding their manners in the presence of the nilaon.

Moccasin congratulated the new recruits and wandered toward the high officer's table where he took his seat next to Atticus.

"Your trainee didn't do very well." Atticus frowned. The leader sipped from his glass. He was drinking whiskey and not his usual wine, which made Moccasin uncomfortable.

Is he angry?

Moccasin eyed the bottle of honey-colored whiskey at the center of the table. "No, he didn't."

Atticus smirked. His glass was quickly emptied and placed down. "Have a drink."

Moccasin looked at his hands, embarrassed. "I'm trying to lay off of the stuff. It's been giving me some rough mornings."

Atticus laughed, "I see." He reached for the bottle. "As for me..." Atticus slowly poured. "...I don't mind another."

Moccasin poured himself wine, and they two clinked their glasses.

The whiskey's lure was difficult to ignore. It took all of his power to resist it, but it always seemed to be there for him.

Bera fell into a chair next to them. "How's everyone doing, tonight?" She noticed the opened bottle and looked sideways at him.

"Feeling a bit tired actually." Atticus squeezed his eyes and took another sip.

"Going to call it a night?" Bera asked, looking pointedly at his now empty glass.

"Nonsense!" Atticus blinked a few times, his face glazed in the candlelight. "The celebration has barely begun."

Moccasin's gaze drifted over the room. He spotted Ben but didn't see Wift. He didn't care for that new recruit. There was no reasoning behind it just that he'd earned to trust his instincts in Hazdrim. Atticus' son at the fort could only mean trouble.

"*Wift is the enemy!*" A familiar voice snarled from over his left shoulder.

He winced sharply and was amazed to see the white Keeper standing behind his chair. It had been decades since he had seen her, although the tortured dreams of her continued to haunt his sleep.

Due to the crowd, he couldn't respond. He tried to look away but was unable to come out of his shock.

Her lip curled. *"He is the host of my enemy. This makes him your enemy."*

"Moc? Are you listening?" Bera asked.

Suddenly freed from the phantom image, he slowly turned to Bera. "No... sorry. What did you say?"

Bera grumbled. "I think we should reduce the number of patrols."

"Yeah, sure." He wasn't able to concentrate. He looked behind to see the Keeper had vanished, and he was able to breathe again.

Atticus coughed. "I think the drink has got the best of me." He stood up on wobbly legs and shook his head. "I'm turning in. Good night."

He left the table and passed through the crowd.

Moccasin shut his eyes. "Can't I leave?"

"No." Bera kicked him from under the table.

"Well, in that case..." He reached for the amber colored bottle, but Bera snatched it away from him.

"Hey!" Moccasin snarled, "You said you wanted a drinking buddy."

"Oh stop. I'm just trying to help you."

Bera held the bottle closer and squinting her eyes, she sniffed it. "Strange."

"Yeah, what's going on with you? You're

actin' weird."

"It smells...off."

"What do you mean?" Moccasin scooted closer. He leaned over to sniff the bottle, however Bera pulled it away from him.

She sniffed it again. "Who drank from this?"

"Atticus was the only one here before I came in." His eyes widened. "Wait, give me the bottle."

He held it up to his nose. A quick sniff brought him to his feet. Moccasin grabbed a soldier walking by. "Find Nilaon Atticus. Quickly!"

Bera stood up as well. "Is it bad?"

Why would someone go to the trouble of poisoning just one bottle?"

Someone is trying to assassinate Atticus.

Unless it was meant for me.

Sprinting Moccasin followed Bera from the table and through the corridors. He remained calm to properly focus and handle the situation, but no amount of calm would prepare him for what they found.

Atticus hadn't made it to his room. He was discovered lying on the corridor floor with thick black foam coming out of his mouth. His eyes were rolled in the back of his head and his body convulsed terribly and then froze. Their nilaon was gone.

Someone had poisoned the whiskey. At that thought, Moccasin's mind began to run through all the scenarios and suspects. Atticus had many enemies, but so did he.

Bera knelt to inspect the nilaon. She looked up at him and shook her head. There were no words. They were both having the same thoughts.

The other drinks were inspected by the three highrindh, and just the one whiskey bottle had been poisoned. All food and beverages had been consumed by everyone at the banquet, and no one else showed signs of illness.

There was no doubt in Moccasin's mind that it had been placed at the high table for him. He was well known for drinking whiskey. Someone had poisoned it...intending to kill him.

Who is trying to kill me?

Whomever it was, their plan had backfired. No one could've known that Atticus would switch from his usual wine and partake of the whiskey. But he had, and now they were without a leader.

There was an assassin among them.

.....

"I don't want excuses!" Moccasin snapped at the fort's steward. "I want names of all the servers, staff, and soldiers who had access to the bottles."

"Moccasin, they are working on it. We all want answers." Bera thanked the steward and sent him away.

Moccasin narrowed his eyes at Bera. "Our

leader of hundreds of years was killed by a poison that was intended for me!" He slammed his fist on the office table. "The only thing we know is that it was sanguis venom."

Sanguis was an animal that resembled a deer with mange. Their fangs secreted a venom that could be made into a poison which was fatal for Nephilim. It would burn its victim from the inside out, causing a painful death. The poison had a sweet floral scent that had been emanating faintly from the one bottle. Atticus, who rarely drank the liquor, wouldn't have noticed any peculiarity. Moccasin was a much more experienced drinker, but he had the wine. The two men had switched their preferred beverages unknowing what that would portend.

"Why should I be calm?" He raked his finger through his untidy hair. "Someone is trying to kill me!"

Bera took a deep breath and slouched into her chair. "We don't know that it was intended for you. There's no way we can know for certain."

"Something is going on here! How can you be so stubbornly blind?" his eyes narrowed. "Unless...unless you think you know who did it!"

Bera stood and turned away from him. "Maybe you need some time off," she muttered.

Grace shook her head and leaned against a wall. "Sanguis poison is illegal and terribly hard to obtain. Someone put a lot of effort into this."

"Thank you!" He pointed to Grace.

Bera countered, "The soldiers will want answers. The whole region will want answers, but first, they need to feel safe. If we say that their leader was murdered...there will be chaos." She intertwined her fingers. "The other regions might seize this opportunity to try and launch an attack while we're disoriented. They would see this as a weakness among our ranks. We need to be stronger than ever. We should say that Atticus consumed too much alcohol and had an accident."

Grace nodded in agreement, "It could even have been a foreign spy sent to poison Atticus. They wouldn't know his drinking habits. That he rarely drinks whiskey."

Moccasin felt panic rise. He knew the whiskey was meant for him. Anyone with intentions to kill Atticus would have poisoned the wine bottle, Atticus' preferred drink. To his mind, there was no other sufficient explanation, and nothing would convince him otherwise.

"It was the enemy! He wants you dead!" The white keeper boomed next to him.

"Shut up." Moccasin muttered.

Bera and Grace exchanged confused glances.

"It was just a thought." Grace shrugged. "It is possible. Right?" She looked to Bera for assistance.

"No. It's not you." Moccasin sighed, "It's nothing." He changed the subject. "Who is going to be temporary nilaon?"

Grace tapped a pencil against her leg. "We can't make this decision without careful thought. I say we don't decide right away. Let's continue working together, just the three of us."

Bera agreed, "Good idea. Once the region grieves properly, we can deliberate. That way we appear strong and unified while still respectful."

In Tavdren tradition, the three highrindh would decide on one of them to be the new nilaon. If two or more highrindh want the promotion, then it would resort to combat.

It usually goes to combat.

Moccasin's least concern was about the new leader. He needed to know who'd want him dead.

The white keeper had been pushing thoughts into his head more frequently. Speaking up from nowhere. Making him paranoid. He now knew why he'd an instant contempt for Jin and for Wift. His instincts were not really his own.

He is host to her enemy.

That makes him my enemy.

And she wants him dead.

He would never touch a drop of alcohol again.

.....

Chapter Thirty-One

Moccasin paced between the row of stalls. "Who'd want me dead?" he quietly asked the horses who eyed him from over their wooden gates.

"Everyone. You're a mage." The white Keeper suddenly appeared perched on a bag of oats.

Moccasin wasn't surprised at her arrival. "Can't you..." He struggled to find the words.

"Turning down the advice of an esteemed keeper? Ungrateful boy. What are you going to do?"

"What is it with you? Can't ya find another heir to mess with, and leave me alone?"

The Keeper came off the bag. Her maroon eyes, her only color, blinked slowly. *"I have only two. And you,"* here she tilted her head at him, *"have more malleable than the other."*

"How are we related, anyway?" Frustrated, he paced away from her. "Ya know what...I don't wanna know."

One problem at a time.

One problem at a time.

She followed him. *"It was the enemy. He tried to poison you. He wants you dead!"*

"You think Wift did this?" He asked yet knowing that Wift was a suspect. "The keeper that is sharing a body with Wift, why do you hate him?"

The keeper flinched. *"My reasons are not your concern."*

"It is my concern because I don't trust you!" Moccasin hissed. "And you need me!"

She snarled back, *"He deserves death. That's all I will say about the matter."*

"What's the keeper's name?"

"Tavious. The keeper who founded Tavdren."

"Let me get this straight. You six keepers, all together have to complete a spell to get back to The Golden Realm?"

"Aurum." She nodded.

"But you're dead...so you all must share a body with a descendant to carry this out."

"That is correct."

"But you," Moccasin pointed to the white keeper, "don't want to go through with the spell? Right? Because having this Tavious keeper dead is worth dying yourself and never returning to your realm?"

"That is accurate. I would rather die eternally here with my host than ascend to the realm with my enemy."

Moccasin ran his hands over his stubbled chin. "So, you want me to kill Wift, Tavious' host, so that the keepers can't make this spell?" He stopped and turned to her. "You are cursing them all here to die with their hosts!"

She nodded. *"Yes, I despise them all."*

Moccasin snarled, "This is demented."

"I chose you specifically for the purpose of killing him. None of the other keepers have chosen a nephilim-magus host. You will catch them by surprise. You're the perfect tool."

Moccasin stared at her. His mouth opened and shut.

She shook her head and marveled. *"You should be honored! The privilege to share your body with me! It's a righteous duty!"*

He slumped against a stall. "Is there any way ya can leave me, and let me try to have a normal afterlife? As normal as possible?"

"I've waited a long time for you to be ready. I've waited longer for revenge on Tavious. You will learn to value my presence. Soon you will require my casting energy. Spell my name in blood to summon me if you ever need me when I have gone quiet. We will learn to get along."

"Spell your name in... I don't even know your name." He looked repulsed.

"Lawan."

"Are you going to keep popping up or are you going quiet, as you have been for the last hundred years?"

"You will see me."

"What do you want me to do with Wift?"

"You need to kill him."

Moccasin leaned against a stall gate. He knew that he couldn't trust everything she'd told him. Without evidence, he wouldn't be certain that Wift was the one behind the poison. She wanted him dead, and it all seemed too convenient.

Is Lawan setting Wift up as the murderer to fuel my anger against him?

In the quiet barn, there came a loud thump against the outside of the wall. Lawan, the white keeper, instantly vanished.

Moccasin silently walked to the entrance and looked around for the source of the sound. A streak of black fabric flashed across a stall window. Someone in a long black hood was running into the forest.

Had they been listening?

Without another thought, he chased after them, but the figure was soon lost among the tangle of trees. The figure easily blended in with the shadows. The cloak had an unfamiliar red stitching going down the back. Moccasin burned the stitching into his memory. He searched the area, but the trail had been lost.

He looked down at his watch. The patrols wouldn't have gone out on patrol at this time. No work shifts were due for hours. Whomever the hooded figure was, they had come to the barn with the intention of spying on him and slipping away into the forest without being seen.

He returned to the barn.

If it was the person who had poisoned Atticus, then his suspicions were growing. Someone was indeed after him, undeterred by Atticus' accidental death.

It could be more than one person.

"Mr. Moccasin?"

He turned to face Ben. The young recruit smiled happily. It had been a few days since the recruits' initiation, and with all the turmoil, they hadn't had a chance to talk.

Moccasin took a calming breath. "What do you want, Ben?"

"Bera sent me to find you."

"Oh." Moccasin collected himself. "I was on a walk. Does she need something?"

"She and Grace finished addressing the assembly. She said that Atticus' death was an accident?" Ben's face was confused as he spoke.

Moccasin replied, "That's as much as we're willing to divulge." No part of him wanted to tell Ben the truth. Instinct told him that the kid probably had a big mouth. The safety of Tavdren was a priority and the highrindh couldn't afford to start a panic.

Ben tilted his head. He looked Moccasin up and down. "Are you okay, Sir? You seem upset."

"I'm fine." He moved past the young man, taking the path back up to the fort.

.....

Moccasin went to Bera's suite. Someone could be waiting in his own. Until he knew more about the poison and now the cloaked figure, he wouldn't rest easy in his chambers.

I am being paranoid.
But with reason!

"Bera." He knocked on her door. "Open up. I am hungry."

A muffled voice came from deep in the suite. "It's unlocked."

He opened the door and went directly to her small kitchen.

"Why didn't you eat in the hall with us?" She asked.

"Why do you think? Someone is trying to poison me!" He snapped, opening a cupboard. "The last place I'll be eating is in the dining hall."

Bera was busy writing something at her desk. She didn't look up. "Take anything except the cheese."

Moccasin grabbed a green apple from a bowl next to the wash sink. He bit into the tart apple and wandered toward her desk.

"What are you doing?" he asked, chewing noisily.

She kept writing. "Just taking notes about

the events before and after Atticus' death."

Moccasin sat at the table and allowed his gaze to drift around her rooms and the general disorder of her suite. Bera had never been one for good housekeeping. Items were stacked on all surfaces, and a thin layer of dust rested upon most objects. A closet door was left ajar in which he could see jackets crammed on a few overburdened hangers.

The sofa is the only clutter-free...
Wait.

Something caught his attention, and his gaze switched back to the closet.

Moccasin cast a sideways look in Bera's direction to see if she was watching him, but she was drawn into her work.

He took another bite of apple and zeroed in on the closet contents.

Just as he'd thought. In the closet, thrown haphazardly, was a solid black cloak. He shifted his body and slowly turned his head to get a better look. The cloak was hooded. It had a red line of stitching running down the length. Red stitching.

Moccasin's eyes widened.

Bera? Bera was the one spying on me?

His heart pounded in his chest.

Did Bera poison Atticus?
Did she try to poison me?

.....

Part Four

.....

O'MERIT KAY

Chapter Thirty-Two

Well over a thousand years ago, Bera Aze woke in a white fabricated object. Her mind was in a dense fog. Her mouth felt dry, and she couldn't focus her eyes on anything but milky white. Slowly she regained feeling in her body.

Breathe.

In and out.

Breathe.

Memory poured into her.

Raiders attacking her family's longhouse. Her running to the entrance with an axe. Smelling the smoke. Eyes burning. Seeing the bodies of her brother and friend in the common space beyond her garden. Her young sister's cries distracting her from the incoming blade.

The shieldmaiden had no time to react. She was dead before her body fell.

Bera tried to control her rushing senses. Every part of her body was screaming. Concern for her family was the only thing in her mind, but her training had prepared her for dangerous and unusual situations. She was alert to something different. Something unfamiliar surrounding her.

Did I die?

Am I in Valhalla?

The soft, white surrounding her abruptly opened, and she tumbled out landing on her bare feet in a battle-ready position. Bera had no weapon, yet she was prepared to fight. She was a Norse shieldmaiden.

The scene before her left her confused. None of her experience prepared her for what awaited.

She was in a very large, brightly lit wooden room. A small group of people huddled together in a far corner. They were looking over a parchment and chatting quietly. One glanced in her direction but didn't approach. Cocoon-like white objects were hanging from low beams. Several had been opened. She looked up and realized that it was from one of these in which she had just emerged.

Five people were standing in the center of the room looking as disoriented as Bera felt. Each had on the same white fabric gown as her. Not one of them spoke. They were sizing up their situation with blank-eyed stares. Vacant. Stunned.

One man broke away from the corner group and approached a younger man in the center of the room. Without any warning, he grabbed the young man's arm and proceeded to lead him to a door. The young man shouted and kicked out but was no match for his captor's size. He was dragged from the room, frantically yelling in an unfamiliar language.

With the young man's cries still ringing in Bera's ears, she didn't sense the threat. Suddenly, she was caught by her arms from behind and pushed toward the same door as the young man. Bera didn't struggle. She was outnumbered and in a foreign environment. Even if she escaped, there was no telling how many people were waiting outside. For the time being she had to cooperate, but she was taking in all the details for a future escape.

Bera would save her strength for a more advantageous moment. Then she would unleash her fury.

"Come with me."

The language her captor spoke was vaguely familiar, although it wasn't Norse. It was an ancient language she'd only ever heard in myths. Stories the elders told around the fires after feasts.

On her way being led out, she turned at the sound of her name. "Bera!"

Torald!

"Torald!" She howled.

He was raising up off the floor underneath an opened white pod. Her brother's rough, wolf-like face beseeched her. "Bera! Where are we? What is this place?"

Bera began to violently struggle against her captor. She was going to get her brother. She elbowed the person who was holding her. "I want my brother!"

The person ignored her. He continued to shove her in the direction of the door.

"Bera! Stay still! I'm coming!" She heard Torald yell.

The memory of Torald's bleeding body flashed in her mind's eye. He'd definitely died in that raid. She remembered seeing his lifeless eyes staring up at her.

This means I am dead, too.

But I don't feel dead!

She was pulled into a smaller stone room where rows of cots were lined against the walls. The man roughly sat her on a bed and bound her hands to the metal rail.

"Bacraut!" Bera spilled a slur of insults as the person left. She scanned the room and saw scared faces looking back at her.

"Let me go!" She screamed, struggling to free herself. "Release me!"

Torald was soon chained to a cot three down from hers. She was filled with a determination to break free of the chains and go to him. *This doesn't feel like Valhalla.*

Torald was her older brother. He had blonde hair and a sturdy build. His soft, brown eyes were different from hers. Bera had dark brown eyes flecked with ruby and long, bright red hair, usually kept in a braid. Now it was loose and fell down her back in tangled waves.

Torald walked with an uncomfortable limp. It was a battle wound, which he'd suffered from too early in his life. His face was scarred and weather-worn from voyages, but Bera saw him as comforting and caring.

Bera also had scars. They were on her forehead, eyebrow, and cheek, and she took pride in them. Scars were a badge of hard-fought battles. She was a shield maiden from Nynorsk. Her family was Aze.

Glanced at her bondage, she realized they was poorly made. With a few tricks, she should be able to break free. All that mattered at the moment was getting to Torald.

Bera's hands turned and twisted the cords. The bonds cut against her wrists, making them blister and ooze with droplets of blood. She gritted her teeth together from the pain.

"Keep working, Bera!" Torald hissed. He

was at his cot working at his bondage in a frenzy. She could see the muscles in his arms bulge with the effort.

This gave her courage. Bera shut her eyes and shouted out a battle cry. And then with one last effort, the cords fell from her wrists.

Hurrying off the cot, she went to Torald. Blood dribbled down her arm as she ran.

"What is happening?" She knelt before him and began to loosen his cords.

"I don't know," Torald whispered. "This can't be Valhalla."

"We have to remain faithful in the gods," Bera replied. He'd been bound with heavier cords, but together they managed to get one loose. "What's our plan?"

"I'm not sure. We need answers," he re-plied.

"Then let's take one of them hostage!"

Torald shook his head. "They don't speak Norse."

"I could understand some of what they said," She explained, twisting the other cord off and freeing him. "With the right number of teeth pulling, we can get them to show us the way out." Bera snarled.

Torald moved his wrists around. They were not as bloody as Bera's. His cool and calm demeanor would prove helpful in their situation. "I think we should wait here for one of them to come back and then-"

"-We take them!"

"Ya. But if they try to put those cords back on me, I will take their eyes out." Torald chuckled and got up from the cot.

"At least we are here together." Bera punched his shoulder.

"Thank the gods." Torald whispered.

It was then that Bera noticed a long jagged, black scar running across the back and side of Torald's head. It was the wound that had killed him. She checked her own body for one but saw nothing. Running her fingers down her neck, she felt a scar straight across her throat.

I was beheaded?

That is a worthy way to go.

Just like grandfather.

.....

The doors opened and seven people entered and began to go down through the room inspecting the prisoners in their row. Bera and Torald were sitting passively on their cots as if still bound. They'd hidden the damaged cord under a cot.

A single guard remained at the door. Torald gave Bera a nearly imperceptible nod and simultaneously they rushed the lone guard. The man was blindsided by having two freed Viking Wakers suddenly attack him. Four of his companions immediately rushed to his aid, and at the end of a fierce struggle, both Bera and Torald were bound with chains on opposite ends of the chamber. Bera was sucking a busted lip.

A larger man in full chain armor approached Bera. He examined her bloody wrists carefully before placing his hands against her ears. His fingers released a warm and colorful mist into her ears and over her face. She felt it traveling inside her. She resisted by holding her breath but eventually was forced to inhale the vapor. When he removed his hands and spoke, Bera was surprised to find out that she could clearly understand his words.

"Welcome to the afterlife. You will not escape, so do not try again. Do you understand?"

Bera nodded, bending over double to tug at her ears with her now securely bound hands. "So, this is Valhalla?" Her eyes widened, hearing that she could speak the language as well as comprehend.

"No."

"But you said it's the afterlife."

"It is. For nephilim."

"So, it's a Valhalla for nephilim? What is a nephilim? Are they tasty?"

The guard tilted his head in confusion. "Uh...no..."

"But you said-"

"This isn't Valhalla." The guard sighed and tried his best to explain. "There is a species called keepers. You have heard myths about them, as they've inspired some of earth's religions with their unnatural, other-worldly characteristics. The keepers procreated with humans, thus creating nephilim." He pointed to her and back to himself. "We are nephilim, and because we aren't fully human, we can't go to the human afterlife. We come here."

"Ya." Bera nodded. "So... this is Valhalla?"

The guard ran his hands down his face. "We are going to be here a while, aren't we?"

"I am hungry."

.....

Chapter Thirty-Three

Bera and Torald sat subdued on the cot and ate what they believed to be smoked pork. They watched everyone else in the holding chamber sitting and eating as they were.

"Which region should we join?" Torald asked, biting off a chunk of meat.

The siblings had just been informed about the five regions and the groups of soldiers who govern each. In a few hours, they'd make their decisions. Afterward, a representative of each region would come to collect the Wakers.

"What do you think of the Challavenge?"

"Too cold. It would be nice to live someplace warm for a change." Torald suggested.

"Ya." Bera thought over the descriptions. "Golovarn, then? It's not cold!"

Torald shook his head. "No. The wildlife would be a problem. Perhaps...Tavdren?"

"I don't like the sound of it."

"But they have a good military. We would do well there, and gain authority!"

"True." Bera liked the idea of a position of leadership.

"We will fight till the day we die and reach Valhalla!"

"But..." She intertwined her fingers. "...we've already died and didn't get to Valhalla." She looked around suspiciously. "Unless this is some test to get to Valhalla!"

"Ya." Torald nodded. "I think you're correct."

.....

Bera's favorite memories of earth were of feasts days. After a raid, the village would join together for a meal with music and stories. One particularly special memory was of the celebration feast of her becoming a shieldmaiden.

The first real meal in the afterlife wasn't as celebratory as what she'd been promised. In Valhalla, there would've been delicacies and festivities. Here, it was unseasoned hares roasted over the campfire on their journey to Tavdren. It was a plain meal like she would've expected on a raid but not her first in the afterlife.

The group sat by the fire's glow, eating, and telling stories of their time on earth. It amused her that no one would tell their death stories. It was taboo here. She was very proud of her death and pleased to see her death scar was on her neck where all could see it. It would be an honor to discuss her magnificent end.

Their escort was a warrior named Atticus. He was brooding and quick-tempered, yet his intense yellow eyes were steady. In general, he was attractive with dark hair and sharp features, though Bera didn't care for him. She sensed that he was weak.

No spine.

Torald didn't like Atticus either. He seemed repulsed by the stone-carved man.

Atticus showed them how to perform casting. It was impressive magic. The cast was colored energy that was used to create weapons and shields. Not every nephilim had the ability to cast, but those that could had a distinct color.

Bera's casting color was a bright red. Atticus explained that the color was a Nephilim's signature, unique to each person. Like a fingerprint.

Torald's color was the light reddish brown of a deer's hide.

During the night, while most had settled in for sleep, Bera sat by the fire practicing casts. A red flicker came from her hands, and she attempted to expand it into a war hammer.

Deeper into the night, when everyone but her was asleep, a blinding, yellow flash of eyes sped past the camp just on the other side of the fire. It was no animal as the eyes were far above the forest floor. Instinctively she reached for her blade, but her hand found none at her side. Not having her Viking short axe caused her to feel unbalanced.

Bera was certain she saw a figure run and hide among the trees. It appeared just in her field of vision looking back at her. She was certain it smiled tauntingly.

Excitement grabbed hold of her, and she bolted after it. With her eyes fixed on the figure, she stumbled on a sleeping Waker bundled in blankets. She didn't stop. Hearing the fleeing figure's jeering laughter caught her mind into a steel trap that was focused only on her goal. Nothing would slow her down.

The creature was black and white except for two gleaming yellow eyes. It was quick, but Bera wouldn't let it outpace her. Once she reached a close distance, she sprung out snatching at it with her hands. However, her fingers slipped through the figure as if it were nothing more than a phantom. To her bewilderment, she fell hard and hit the forest ground with a heavy thud.

Bera grunted and tried to stand. A bit dazed, she slipped again and lay looking about for the black and white phantom. To her surprise, it had stopped and turned back to her with hands on its hips. Mocking her. She could now see that the figure was a young male.

Cocky, self-confidence emanated from him as he strutted to stand over her. He was wearing regal, yet poorly fitted clothing, obviously created for a larger man. He appeared to be wearing his father's clothes. By the size of this boy, he couldn't have been older than fifteen.

"Why did you stop? You almost caught me," it said, giving her a boastful grin.

She saw that like a ghost, he was partially transparent. The phantom had the glowing yellow eyes of a hellcat.

"What are you? A demon?" Bera stood, wiping dirt from her cheek. She was angry at herself for falling and not catching her opponent but wasn't at all baffled by what she now faced. Finding herself in the presence of a ghost, or demon, wasn't outside the realm of possibility for a Viking shield maiden who'd been raised on myth and legend.

"Demon?" He took a hand from his hip and brushed his short and curly hair back off his forehead, revealing long and pointed ears. *"I'm not going to take offense."*

"You should." She mumbled under her breath. "Who are you?"

"My name is Challen." He bowed low in an elegant, courtly gesture.

"That's a stupid name. What are you? Answer me!" Bera demanded rolling her bruised shoulder.

"We all have our opinions. As for who I am, let me just say that I'm very insulted that my own decedent chose Tavdren over my region, Challavenge. I'm a keeper."

"So... you're a ghost?"

"That's rude." He clicked his tongue, disapprovingly. "I might be dead, but I am definitely not a ghost."

She paused. "Wait...you are the keeper I'm related to? You?" She was disappointed in his appearance.

"Of course!" Challen scoffed. *"Couldn't you tell? We share the same good looks."*

"No." Bera frowned at his familiar manner. "We don't."

"How *does my favorite granddaughter like the Nephilim Realm?"*

Bera shrugged and picked a leaf from her hair. "It's not Valhalla." she narrowed her eyes. "How could you be my grandfather? You're a child."

"I'm older than I appear." Challen stood up straight and adjusted his long sleeves. *"I need your help, Bera. I need you to do something for me. Can I count on you?"*

"I don't think so. You're boring me already." Bera turned to go back to camp, yet she could hear Challen following her.

"My fellow keepers and I have been banished

here. The only way we can go back to our realm is through a spell."

"How can you do a spell? You're a ghost." She scoffed over her shoulder.

"Exactly that! I can't. None of us can. That is part of the curse." The young keeper floated through her and stood in her path. Bera staggered at the icy feeling. *"The spell requires all keepers to be present for it to work properly."*

"You do not have a body!" Bera stuck her hand through his torso.

The young keeper laughed at her. *"You are funny, Bera. That is why I have chosen you to be my host."*

"Do what?"

"Every keeper needs a body to perform the spell." He attempted to pat her head, but his hand went through her. *"And you are my lucky grand-daughter!"*

Bera flinched.

"The Keeper Sundra and her host are already here. I imagine they are in Drundra since that's her region. By now Sundra will have sensed my illustrious presence."

Bera looked sideways at him, "So you are going to give me a warning before you take control of me, or not?"

"Well...my spirit went into you the moment you died." Challen cut her off before she could respond. *"But until now I've been in 'hibernation'. This is when I observe through your eyes and stay*

hidden inside of you. In another dimension. Right now, I am being 'active'. Which is when my soul can wander within a certain proximity from our shared body. It allows me to communicate with you and move around. Only you are affected by my active state. Hence the reason why you can see and hear me, and others cannot."

Challen flexed and floated through a tree. *"You're not surprised by all of this?"*

Bera shrugged. "It's not the craziest thing I've heard today." She rubbed her head. "You're like my Valkyrie."

"No. Well, you know what...sure. I am your Valkyrie." He conceded. *"The point is, we are going to be sharing a body until the day the keepers reunite and our hosts perform the spell. Then I can go home to my world. And you can...plunder this one."*

She looked around the forest. "Well, then we just need to go get these keepers."

"Let's take this one step at a time. Which is getting you to Tavdren."

"Highrindh Atticus is taking us there. We should probably return before anyone awakens and becomes suspicious," Bera replied, noticing the sky had turned the pink and purple of early dawn.

Challen nodded, and silently they walked to camp. Bera followed the ghostly man. She didn't fully understand everything her keeper-grandfather had told her, but from what he'd said, they were stuck together.

Can I tell Torald about this?

The campfire flames flickered through the trees. As Bera approached the campsite, she noticed that Challen slowly began to fade from her sight.

He must be going into hibernation.

When she returned, a few Wakers were up and cooking another hare for the morning meal. She found the tree where she'd left her few possessions and watched the camp with tired eyes. Torald was snoring softly in his blanket roll.

.....

Chapter Thirty-Four

Bera and Torald walked at the rear of the group. She lifted her head to look at the clear sky. It was a cool day.

"Think we will have good consultants?" she asked.

"Of course! Now stop trying to distract yourself. We need to practice casting so we can master the skill." Torald scolded.

Bera made a small cast. She wished Challen would show himself, as she had many more questions now that she'd had time to think.

"We are almost at the fort!" Atticus announced from the front and held up his right hand. The group came to a stop. Eight Nephilim, including Bera and Torald, had decided to join Tavdren's military group at the fortress.

Atticus had told them about the other two highrindh, Cossy and Jin. And their nilaon, Alleari. Bera desperately wanted to meet Alleari and make a strong first impression as Atticus had described the Tavdren nilaon as a strong ruler.

"You will see that we're constructing two towers and may be asked to assist in this work effort as your task."

Atticus led the group along the forest path when unexpectedly, amongst the trees, as if it had grown up in the forest, was a massive fortress. Bera had never seen anything like it in her travels as a shieldmaiden. It would hold many of the Nordic longhouses inside its walls.

Homesickness came upon her and was excruciatingly painful. Having Torald by her side had been comforting, but she was overcome with the finality of never seeing her earthly home again. Others weren't so lucky. They were alone in the realm with nothing and no one. She would remember that whenever she succumbed to this homesickness.

"It's massive," Torald whispered in awe as they walked through the heavy wooden front doors.

Bera nodded in agreement. Her loose red hair blew across her face, and she tucked it behind her ear.

Many people were bustling in through the same entrance as the Waker group. They carried market produce and goods to sell to the inhabitants. Some transported construction stone and supplies. They all greeted Atticus formally but paid very little, if any, attention to the Wakers.

Taking a deep breath, Bera raised herself to her full stature. She had confidence in herself and her abilities, although she wished that her shield was with her.

Nothing makes a more imposing impression than a Nordic shield wielded by a fierce shieldmaiden.

Torald came along with the group. The pain in his leg had become more pronounced from the long journey, but he was a Viking warrior and managed to summon his strength. Torald wouldn't allow the limp to set him apart.

After many turns through the labyrinth fortress, they arrived at a grand courtroom. A woman with long white-blonde hair cascading over her shoulders was sitting elegantly on a wooden throne. She wore brown striped markings on her austere face. A set of brown armor covered her slim figure. Intelligent blue eyes regarded the arrival of the new Wakers.

This must be the nilaon, Alleari.

Atticus took them to the chairs set before the dais and walked up to sit next to Alleari and two others. Bera guessed that the two were the other highrindh, Jin and Cossy. Bera took in her surroundings. The great room was made of stone and was filled with Tavdren soldiers seated in long rows. There was much noise coming from the audience.

Alleari gracefully stood and walked to the edge of the platform. She lifted a single delicate finger, and the room became completely still.

"Welcome all." Her slow, feminine voice was mesmerizing. "Thank you to Highrindh Atticus, who has brought us eight potential recruits."

The soldiers in the grand hall stomped their feet in agreement filling the cavernous space with a raucous that reached the rafters.

Alleari smiled and the room grew still once more. "Before we assign the consultants, I would like to address the rumors. Challavenge has indeed lost their nilaon. They will likely assign a new one soon. This however does not affect us in the slightest." She scanned her people.

"Now that is settled, onto the assigning." She returned to her throne and sat down. "As tradition dictates, the one who guides them has the first choice. Highrindh Atticus brought the Wakers; he's earned the right."

Atticus bowed formally to her and walked to the edge of the dais. His decision was brief. A glance to the Wakers reminded him of the time he spent guiding them. He'd seen their potential.

"You." He pointed to a well-built young

man who'd shown casting skills early on in their journey.

Highrindh Jin selected Bera. Highrindh Jin wore rose pink armor and had piercing pink eyes. Her jet-black hair and pink complexion made her appear harsh, but Bera's experience with shieldmaidens told her that there would be much more to her than her appearance.

Torald was eventually selected by a soldier of rank. Training would be hard because of his leg, although they'd both been encouraged to learn that casting while draining, required more mental strength than physical.

"The Wakers and Consultants will meet tomorrow. Tonight, they will rest, and acclimate to their new home." Alleari looked the Waker recruits each one in the eye. "Guides will escort you to your chambers." With that said, the nilaon dismissed them.

Everyone, including the highrindh, left without saying a word. The room emptied as if by ghosts, so silently did the soldiers file out into the corridor. It was obvious that this nilaon was feared and respected.

.....

The quarters were relatively small but comfortable, more than what Bera had been used to in Nynorsk. Torald's room was beside hers.

Bera prepared for bed in the clothes she'd been provided. She needed to get plenty of sleep for the challenging day ahead. The next day would be full of new information and training, and Bera was determined to take advantage of every opportunity to advance.

"Bera, this place is so small!" Challen complained as he floated in and out of the walls. *"Of course, Tavdren would allow such small quarters. They are animals."*

"I'm a recruit. It's only fair that we get the worst quarters. Where I come from, one must earn a bed. By earn, I mean fight. It's a rite of passage. By comparison, this is a palace." She sat on the edge of her straw bed and patted the mattress.

Her keeper was immature with a temperament like that of a child. Challen groaned. *"Don't even get me started on-"*

Bera rolled her eyes and threw one of her boots. The boot went through Challen.

He gasped, gravely offended. *"That is rude!"*

"Just be quiet. I need sleep." She crawled under the covers of the bed. Having not slept the night before, fatigue hit her instantly. "Begone, ghost."

She threw the other boot. The keeper shrieked and faded into a wall.

.....

The next morning, seeing the training room was already occupied, they found another place to work. Jin took Bera outside to a training field. It was behind the fort and overgrown with high grass. Not ideal, according to Jin, but they had it to themselves.

Bera had a chance to observe the surrounding land. The birch forest was surprisingly dark. The tree's limbs and dark sky drew shadows in the forest.

On the far edge of the field, three deer leaped over a dead tree and raced into the thicket. Bera watched them disappear into the dark forest. It reminded her of hunts that she'd been on as a little girl.

Jin brought her back to the present, asking with a sharp tone. "Were you listening?"

"I was distracted."

Jin frowned. "I asked you to show me a shield-cast."

Bera nodded. She took a deep breath, planted her feet, and focused her mind's eye on the shield from her home. She summoned a shield-cast.

"How's this?" Bera was impressed with herself.

"Decent."

A bird flew from a tree limb and called out to its mate. Bera jerked her head at the sound. Her concentration was broken, and the shield quickly faded away.

Jin rubbed her forehead. "You need to work on concentration. A cast requires full attention. There will be plenty of distractions in battle. You must learn to overlook it all if you want to live."

Is this puny woman telling me how to battle?
I will take her right now.

"I'm sorry." Bera dipped her head respectfully.

"I expect you to fix this," Jin said with a bit of a snarl. "Fix it."

Bera nodded eagerly and tried to repeat the cast, but by the time she summoned another shield-cast, Jin was already walking back to the castle. "We'll meet in the courtyard this afternoon. Spend the day working on your concentration."

"But-"

"Focus!"

Bera's eyebrows furrowed. The whole exchange was insulting. She drew an axe-cast, bright red and pulsing. The cast was strong at first, but after a few seconds, it became weak and pale.

Casting was taking a lot out of her mentally. She needed to master it quickly to make an impression on the highrindh and niloan. Bera stomped her foot on the ground, shouting a few Norse words out of frustration.

Challen fell from a tree not far from her. The ghostly figure slid right through a rock. *"I'm trying to enjoy nature!"* he said, pretending to brush leaves from his cloak.

"Oh, shut up."

"You're being nasty." Challen adjusted his

baggy shirt and walked to her. He put his hands on his hips and stood heroically.

"Where is that little consultant of yours?"

"She is making me work on concentration."

"Concentration? You?"

Bera scoffed, "Ya. She says I get distracted too easily. We'll see who's distracted when I take her job."

"No. No. No grandchild of mine is going to be criticized by some thick-skulled Tavdren highrindh with a bad attitude." He walked through her.

Bera shook herself. "First, never do that again." She waved her arms at him with the hope of scaring him off. "Second, she's here to help me pass my initiation. I can't get angry at her for giving advice."

"Perhaps. But there's a difference between advice and trying to keep someone busy so you can run off and do something illicit and forbidden." Challen examined his nails and cast a sideways glance at Bera.

She blinked in confusion. "Illegal? Do you think she's off doing something? Right now?"

"Maybe." The Keeper shrugged. He tried to lean against a tree but fell through. His black and white lips twitched, and a smug smile spread across his face. *"I'm sure you'll figure it out."*

.....

Chapter Thirty-Five

"What do you mean?"

"My consultant said I shouldn't go through with the initiation." Torald leaned his bulky frame against a wall in Bera's quarters. His eyes were bloodshot and exhausted. "He says I'm not able to focus on casts properly in battle."

Bera grabbed a bottle of mead off a table. She twisted the cork out and poured it into two cups. "It's your choice. If you don't feel comfortable, you don't have to go through with the initiation."

"But that's the reason why we came. To be warriors again!"

She gave him one of the cups. "We can always leave."

Torald shook his head and accepted the drink. "That would be giving up." He took a few gulps.

"It's not quitting if your life is in danger. You could train to be something else. You know, provide another service." Bera sipped her mead. "Maybe if you had quit before, you would still be able to use your leg properly." She teased playfully.

Torald glanced at her threateningly. "I don't regret earning my injury."

"You shouldn't regret it." She chugged the rest of her drink. "It was honorable."

A day did not go by where she regretted earning her scars. No soldier should be ashamed of a mark they earned while protecting their people.

"It's your choice."

Torald finished his drink and sat with his sister for a good while. "I don't know what to do. Things were easier on earth. With father, mother and Tove. What happened to Tove? Mother was gone by the time I got to her."

"Tove was crying in her room. If she died, wouldn't she be in the realm with us?" Bera asked.

"I suppose," Torald nodded. "What about

Mother? She isn't here."

"I don't want to think about this." She fetched another bottle. Bera had a very high tolerance of alcohol in the Nordic tradition.

"I'm sorry."

"We can talk tomorrow. I should go to sleep."

Torald rose to his feet and gave her a quick hug before leaving her room.

Bera finished the mead and climbed into bed.

"Your brother shouldn't go through with this."

In the darkness, Challen's whisper spooked her. He held his hands up submissively. *"Sorry."*

"Torald can take care of himself."

.....

Bera made a shield-cast and held it for Jin to view.

Jin nodded. "Very good."

A twig snapped behind them causing Bera to jump. She spun around with a war-hammer cast. It was Atticus.

Jin met Atticus as he came into the ring and said, "Alleari wants to see the highrindh."

"Practice your offensive casts." Jin patted Bera's back and left with him.

Bera watched the two walk to the rear entrance. She sat on a log and tried to summon more complex casts. Her favorite was the war-hammer. It reminded her of home.

"Those two are not going to a meeting."

She startled. "Why do you keep sneaking up on me?" Then it hit her what Challen had said. "Wait...what do you mean?"

"Did you see those looks? No one goes to a meeting looking like this-" Challen stared over her shoulder, mimicking their amorous expressions. *"They are a couple."*

"Ya?" Bera looked at their retreating backs. They were almost at the fort and were a tad too close with their shoulders nearly touching.

"It's forbidden for highrindh to be coupled with each other."

Bera absorbed her cast. "Forbidden, huh? This information could come in handy. But I'll need proof."

Challen smiled. *"I think I know how to get it."*

.....

Bera placed strips of raw meat in the cages of the Tasmanian Tigers. The large creatures were trained for battle and protection. Her job at the fort was to train and care for them.

One of the Tasmanian Tigers bounded over and began to feast. Its fur bristled with happiness. She slipped her fingers into the cage and stroked its head gently. Its tail vigorously wagged like a tower banner.

"Good boy."

"I thought I was on morning duty today?" For once an unexpected voice didn't rattle her.

She was getting used to surprise visitors.

Glanced over her shoulder, she saw Rocus striding into the kennel. Unlike the other recruits, Atticus' consultee looked to well-rested.

"Your duty is tomorrow morning." Bera corrected.

"The initiation is tomorrow morning."

"Right." She dropped the rest of the meat in the feed bowl. "So, you'd better wake up early."

Rocus looked around quickly to see if anyone else was nearby. He lowered his tone. "Do you know what the initiation is? My friend said something disturbing. I don't know if he's speaking the truth or not."

Bera narrowed her eyes. "It has to do with casting combat...yeah?"

"Yes. He said we are going to be pitted against prisoners."

"Prisoners?"

"That's what I heard. I wanted to see if you knew."

Bera straightened her posture. Usually, depending on the crime, criminals were banished. Never to be seen again. They only locked the most dangerous ones up for execution. "Is your friend trustworthy?"

"I believe so."

She narrowed her eyes, thinking of Torald. "That is a problem."

"So..." Rocus looked disturbed. "...you think it's true?"

"I don't know."

.....

Bera grabbed Torald's shoulders and turned him sharply to face her. "Torald!"

"What's happened?" He cried.

She shook his shoulders roughly. "You can't go through with the initiation."

"Why do you say this now?"

She explained what she'd discovered. As she spoke, she realized that she should've asked who the source was. All this panic might be for nothing.

Torald took a minute to think it all over. "Who told you this?"

She scratched her neck awkwardly. "...I don't think I should say. They wouldn't like it if it came back to them."

"That's fair, but also unreliable."

"But what if it's true?" She lowered her tone to a whisper and shook him again. "You could be killed!"

Torald yanked himself out of her grip and stalked away from his sister. "You are treating me like a boy! I'm a Nordic Viking!"

Bera replied softly, "Not here, you're not." But Torald was leaving her and didn't hear.

Challen appeared and attempted to pat her shoulder.

She stared down the hallway after Torald, and her unease grew.

What if he is hurt?

Why is he mad at me for warning him?

.....

Chapter Thirty-Six

Bera double-checked her armor. Jin had dropped her in the preparation rooms and left without a backward glance to find her seat in the gallery. Bera was fine with that. She preferred a moment to herself. Bouncing on the balls of her feet she began chanting a Nordic war cry.

The best training she'd received was from Challen. Jin would often take off halfway through a lesson leaving her alone in the field. Luckily, she had her keeper-grandfather to teach her advanced casts.

She was the first one to go which was a

blessing and a curse. Bera could get it over with quickly, however, she wouldn't be able to see the wounds her peers received. There would be no warning on what was to come. It was similar to embarking on a sea voyage to raid a new territory.

"You must be careful. For both of us." Challen warned as he weaved nervously in and out of the walls.

Bera's armor clanked as she moved. It had taken some time getting used to the heavy armor. She'd had only leather armor in her old life.

"Well, I don't have a choice, do I?" She grabbed an axe off of the wall. "Why did you leave your home? If you are so anxious to return?"

"Tavious and Lawan fought. Four of us chose sides." He stared at the ground. *"This displeased The Creator, so all six of us were banished to earth where over time our earthly bodies died. Now that we're here in Hazdrim, our only hope to get back is through you and the other five hosts. The one who could stop us is Lawan. She will do anything to destroy Tavious, even if that means we never return home."*

Challen moved the conversation along a different path. *"Why don't you make an axe-cast instead of dragging that heavy thing around?"* The ghostly keeper attempted to poke the axe.

"I'm used to wielding physical objects. The shield-cast is nice, but I like the weight of an axe."

She swished the metal blade in circles above her head. "It just feels right."

"Whatever you say."

Bera continued swinging the axe in patterns to warm up. She was slightly confused. Everyone said that there were only five keepers. No one talked about the keeper named Lawan that Challen had mentioned.

A guard opened the doors to a dark chamber. He gestured for Bera to follow, and she walked into the chamber confidently.

The room was completely dark inside, although she could feel the cold gazes of the Tavdren spectators in the gallery. She summoned a cast to help guide her way. Challen scooted close to her and hissed in her ear. *"I have a bad feeling about this. You know what's coming, right?"*

Bera rolled her eyes and waved him off. "I don't see anything."

"Yeah. That's why I'm nervous."

She formed a larger cast, illuminating a wider area. The two stared into the dark. A shiny object reflected the cast light, but she was unable to ascertain what it was. Keeper and host exchanged questioning looks.

"Let's see what I've gotten myself into."

"What you've gotten us into. If you die, I'm gone. For good. I won't be able to go home." Challen's yellow eyes widened with fear.

Bera attempted to reassure Challen. "I know how to battle. Trust me." She whispered.

A loud crash alerted them to metal cages. They gleamed red in the glow of her cast as she drew near. An occupant of one cage was rattling the bars to get out.

"Dangerous and creepy." Challen shuddered.

Bera pulled her axe into a ready position and felt the familiar adrenaline pump through her veins. She hadn't felt the battle rush in far too long, but she was ready. "Let's go!"

Challen screamed.

Bera swerved around Challen and proceeded cautiously to the mysterious cages. Tiny tablets were placed on each. Challen pointed to one of the cages. It had her name on it.

"Looks like that's for you."

"Yup."

She slowly approached the cage. There was a very large man inside. His scars had disfigured his features; however, she could still see the once handsome face.

"Son of a beiskaldi!"

Rocus had been right.

We are paired with prisoners.

I have to warn Torald!

.....

Chapter Thirty-Seven

Several hundred years had passed when Bera stood in front of Atticus' desk, "What do you need, Bera?" He groaned. "I've barely settled into this new position."

To her disappointment, Atticus had replaced Alleari as nilaon. The hex who'd assassinated her by tricking Alleari to commit suicide had been captured and was awaiting execution in the dungeon. Bera had doubts about whether the hex was truly guilty, however, she kept this to herself. Atticus was the last person Bera wanted in that position, but then she'd found a way to make it benefit her.

"I know you and Jin are together," Bera said outright and waited for Atticus' reaction.

He slowly looked up to see if she was bluffing.

"And unless you give me the highrindh position...I will tell the other highrindh."

It was a risk, this push for power. Now was the time to use her information to the best effect. Since Torald's demise at his initiation, she'd become obsessed with advancing to leadership in Tavdren. Bera had gone to and would go to any length, which included, bribery, blackmail, and death threats when necessary.

Recalling the memory of her late brother struck a sharp pain through her, but she forced it aside. "Having a relationship with a fellow highrindh is not permitted. The charges would be enough to remove both of you. The highrindh that you had to battle for this seat will not take this lightly."

Atticus' eyes ran over her face, searching her. "How did you..."

"Not important." She was unmoving. "Are you going to give me the promotion of highrindh?"

Atticus' expression hardened. He had his own nephilim in mind for highrindh. Someone loyal to him. He knew that Bera wasn't the ideal candidate and would certainly cross him again. "I won't be blackmailed."

"And yet here we are." She frowned. "And

if you are wondering if there is a way to dispose of me, understand this," she leaned onto his desk and whispered, "I have this information ready to be made public should something unfortunate happen to me."

"You are playing a dangerous game, Bera."

"Highrindh Bera." She corrected him.

There was a quiet pause as the leader considered his options. He had none, and they both knew it. "I need your word that you will bury this."

"Oh, Atticus. I've kept your little secret for seven hundred years. I can be discreet when I wish." She smiled. "You'll find me to be an agreeable highrindh."

The two agreed, and Bera escorted herself out. Her plan had worked perfectly. She knew that Atticus would come to trust her as a highrindh one day. All Tavdren would come to know her as a great highrindh.

Challen walked quietly next to her. He'd learned of her ambition in the long time he had been with her and knew that the obsessive drive to achieve was her way of dealing with the loss of Torald. Bera had never recovered.

He followed Bera outside.

Over the centuries the building had gradually transformed into a massive fortress with two high towers. Even though they were technologically behind earth, the construction was impressive.

Earth was hundreds of years ahead of Hazdrim in technology and science. Nephilim knew this because the newest Wakers had difficulties adjusting to an older way of living. Each group of Wakers had a longer transition period because earth had made advancements in transportation, communication, and medicine. The nephilim regions were slow to catch up.

Bera spent her time training the guard Tasmanian Tigers. They were domesticated now and would respond to her commands. She enjoyed being with the animals. It was simple. When she gave an order, they obeyed and were rewarded.

It wasn't long before all of the Tavdren fortress heard of her promotion. Jin and Dulveron, the other two highrindh, found her in the kennels.

"Congratulations Bera," Jin said, trying to appear genuine. Bera noted that the smile didn't reach her eyes.

"I look forward to working with you," Dulveron added.

Bera returned their false smiles. "Thank you." Her goal was to appear completely unthreatening. She could see that it worked on Dulveron, but not on Jin.

Her former consultant couldn't disguise her fury. The flashing pink eyes exposed her emotions. If anyone could threaten her, it was Jin. Bera understood how dangerous Jin could be and all that she was capable of. It was clear that Atticus had told Jin of Bera's threat.

"I assume you'll be getting the new group of Wakers? It's tradition for a new highrindh to represent Tavdren."

"Correct." Bera nodded. The idea of confronting memories of her Waking and that time with Torald sickened her. Those thoughts were best kept buried.

The Waker Facility was located directly in the center of the mainland. It was now a sweeping campus with rooms that contained more waking pods as the years had passed. No one outside of the Waker facility knew how the pods worked. This was confidential information fiercely protected by the physician's cult-like rules. The Waking was annual, although there was a rumor that the Waking could be moving to once every decade.

"When do I leave?"

"In a month."

Challen smirked at her side. *Didn't think this all the way through, did you?"*

.....

Bera had been a highrindh for a month, with the notam on her hand to show her rank, when she departed for the Waking. The journey to the Waking Center had been long and dull, but she had Challen to keep her company. She had only a vague memory of the building so was therefore surprised to discover that it was a sterile, sprawling structure with drab gray stone walls. It was built along the base of a hill with its lower levels carved into the earth.

The Waking Center was home to the secretive physician's cult, but from outside the building was so prosaic that any passerby would have had difficulty envisioning the activities within. This was the desired effect.

Bera and Challen explored the waking chamber. Ignoring strict warnings, she placed her hand on one of the white pods. It might have been her imagination, but she felt certain it was pulsating. The white fabric wasn't translucent, yet there were the familiar shapes of elbows and knees protruding from the pods. Some were slightly moving, revealing their contents as a baby moves in the womb.

"This place bothers me," Challen whispered as he turned away from the pods.

She teased him. "Toughen up."

The highrindh and doctors were talking in separate groups at the opposite ends of the waking chamber. The physicians regarded the highrindh with condescension while the highrindh were suspicious of the doctors and their secrets.

This was routine for everyone but Bera. Only she was new to this gathering.

"So, the doctors just cut the side and they fall out? How do they get clothes?"

"I don't know. Sundra, the keeper who

founded Drundra, might. She had a connection to one of the early Waker Physicians. If anyone knows, it would be her."

Bera could distinguish the other region's representatives. The highrindh guides looked bored and ready to move on. They wore their region's armor and bore the highrindh brand. It was clear that they were uninterested in meeting Bera. Tavdren highrindh were generally respected but not well-liked.

One doctor broke from the group and announced for everyone to gather.

"It's starting." She and Challen rejoined the others as a physician began laying out instructions on what was to transpire.

Bera observed from the rear. She remembered her Waking experience, being chained to the cot and feeling disoriented. She had relied on Torald in those early days. Now it was Challen. Bera pushed the crippling memories aside.
No reason to focus on what was.

Improvements had been made for the Wakers since her time. Each Waker now received their own examination room and were no longer bound to cots in a common chamber. The physicians treated the Wakers as patients and considered their emotional health to be equally as important as their physical well-being. The facility hadn't only grown in size but was also brightly lit and modern in appearance and practice.

The Waking began. Pods were opened at a slow pace, allowing the inhabitants time to find their legs. This was done under close observation by the staff. One particular Waker who was released from a cocoon landed on the floor with a heavy thud. The young man lay dazed for a moment before terror overwhelmed him. He appeared to be a teen but was enormous in size. This was quietly remarked upon by the doctors as they determined which guard to assist his recovery.

Challen's eyes widened. *"Oh, no!"*

"Hmm?" Bera was fascinated with the transition on the Waker's face as he awkwardly processed this new environment. She must've looked the same way.

Highrindh and physicians had been watching me, too.

Challen moved in front of her, grabbing her attention. *"We need to leave."*

Bera slipped away from the group so she could speak openly with Challen without raising suspension. "Challen what's going on?" She demanded, peeking over his shoulder to get a better view of the Wakers.

"That Waker... that young man is Lawan."

"Am I supposed to understand that?"

"Lawan. She's a keeper. Not a friendly one!" he hissed *"She's the reason we were banished. She is extremely dangerous!"*

.....

Chapter Thirty-Eight

Bera and Challen sat on a bench in the visitor's common room. She intertwined her fingers. "What should we do?"

"Hope that he goes to a different region, so we won't have to deal with him until we absolutely have to."

"And if he chooses Tavdren, what then?"

Challen held his head in his hands. *"I don't want to be near her. She's very hostile. I need the other keepers here before... I can't manage her alone."*

"Aren't you a god or something?"

"A minor deity," he corrected. Then scoot-

ing in close to her, he confessed. *"She scares me."*

Bera knew there was a keeper in Drundra. "Maybe we could have Sundra's host take him...her?"

"Only if he chooses Drundra."

She stood and began pacing. "What do we do? Can we eliminate him and save us the trouble?"

"Absolutely not!" Challen was horrified at the idea. *"All six keepers must be present, with our hosts, to conduct the spell."* Challen sighed. *"You know, Bera, violence isn't the solution to all problems."*

"That's what you say!" Bera sat back down. "Maybe we should try speaking with him. Her. It's possible that he doesn't even know about Lawan."

"And what will you do if he doesn't know about her? If she hasn't approach him already, she will."

"It depends." Bera jumped up. "Let's find his examination room."

Challen led the way using the same keeperial instincts that had warned him of Lawan's arrival in the waking chamber. The keepers had an innate sense of each other's presence. He would find the boy, however he wasn't prepared to confront the keeper, no matter what Bera had planned. And he definitely wasn't comforted by the small dagger-cast she'd made. She had it ready in case Lawan's host was dangerous, or if someone needed stabbing.

Bera followed Challen through the hall-ways until he stopped abruptly at a door. For the first time, Bera saw Challen snarl. She'd never viewed her keeper as a warrior. At that moment, as he was steeling himself for what lay on the other side, she could see the power he wielded and was impressed.

As Bera was going to the door, the knob turned suddenly, and the door was pushed into them by a doctor. Bera stepped out of the way before colliding with the medic.

"Highrindh Bera, may I help you?" The doctor asked suspiciously. "These halls are for physicians only."

"The patient in that room...who is he?" She narrowed her eyes.

The lady replied, "I can't divulge that information."

"It's important."

"I'm certain it is, but it's also against protocol."

Challen growled silently, *"I'll be back."* He faded through the wall.

"You need to leave," the doctor mumbled nervously and ducked past the highrindh. "I have other exams to get to."

At this point, Bera spotted keys that were attached to the medic's belt. When she moved around her, Bera's hand shot out, but in that instant, the doctor unfortunately slipped away.

Leaving Bera empty-handed.

"So close." Bera gritted her teeth. Challen's description of Lawan's host was all she would have. She loitered in the hallway, smiling and nodding when anyone approached. Ten minutes passed before Challen reappeared. His expression was unreadable.

She whispered, "How was it?"

"Let's go somewhere private. You'll have many questions."

The two went upstairs to Bera's temporary lodgings.

As they climbed the stairs, she demanded, "Tell me."

Challen refused to speak until they were safely in her rooms where he sat cross-legged on the bed. *"He's definitely Lawan's host. No doubt about that."*

"I assume he didn't see you?"

"You're the only one who can."

"Then what's wrong?"

Challen was puzzled. *"I don't know. Very hard to read. He's a very big guy. And quiet. Possibly still shocked from waking. His nephilim-casting abilities will be strong. I think there might be some magus blood."* He snorted. *"Leave it to Lawan."*

Bera had to search through her knowledge. She knew very little about the magus kind. "Those are the ones who can control senses?"

"Not control as much as manipulate," Challen explained.

"Isn't that just as bad?"

"Depending on their strength and how much they practice." Challen's yellow eyes blinked. *"Lawan picked him for a purpose, and I don't want to know what that is."* He looked her in the eyes. *"He will be dangerous."*

A long, disturbing silence followed while they both considered what this new information meant.

Bera had always thought of Challen as a blessing. He wasn't demanding, and he wouldn't force her into helping him go home. It was her choice to proceed.

Challen was uncertain how he should guide Bera through what was sure to be a difficult relationship with the new keeper, Lawan. Her presence here was unexpected and not what he wanted to take on alone.

"Do you think they are already connected? You came to me on my second night here."

"I'm not sure. But he didn't know of my presence in his room. That's an indication that she isn't actively with him, because Lawan would have warned him of my presence. Lawan is secretive and likes to take her time. I doubt she would even tell him about the keeper's plan to return to our realm. She was never cooperative. If Lawan talks to him, it would be lies."

"So, he won't even be aware that Lawan is a part of him?"

"It must be her plan to wait. Knowing her,

she will only approach him when she has decided to act."

"Because she will want to stop the keepers from going back to the Golden Realm?"

"Correct. She will start to use him then. When she has a reason."

"How will we know when that is?"

"When all other keepers arrive and begin to unite. That will draw her out. Or when we find people dying for mysterious reasons. It could go either way."

"I've known people like that." Bera shrugged.

"I know you do. That's why I chose you."

.....

"All those for Tavdren, gather here!" Bera shouted, making a red cast to alert them of her whereabouts. Challen stood at her side.

A small group soon began to form in their midst. They were a mixed group of male and female Wakers. It jarred her, although she was quick to hide it, to see the large young man join her group. He towered over the group and looked at her with narrowed eyes.

The Lawan host had chosen to live in Tavdren.

"This isn't good." Challen sighed.

"You've made that clear."

Lawan's host was a handsome with silver hair and eyes. His skin was tanned from a life of work outdoors. She could make out the edges of a death scar emerging from his shirt collar up onto his neck.

The most unusual feature, and what caught her interest immediately, were his eyes. The pure silver color was unexpected, and even if she hadn't already known about the keeper within, the stormy color hinted at something buried but alive.

His eyes were squinting as if struggling to see. She surmised he had a disability, which was uncommon in nephilim. In fact, she'd never met a nephilim who couldn't see well. On earth her friend Halfdan had lost an eye in battle, however, this did not appear to be the same. Lawan's host carried an internal wound to the eyes.

She swiftly turned and withdrew her cast. "Let's go," she announced in her heavy Norse accent.

It was not five minutes before Lawan's host came to her. "Ma'am?"

"Yes?" Bera looked around. Challen hissed in her ear that Lawan's host was approaching and then he quickly vanished.

"I have some questions." The man drawled in a slow, smooth voice. The accent wasn't what she'd expected.

It would be wise to befriend him and make him at ease, but the very idea of Lawan in a magus host was not comforting, especially with Challen leaving her in this first meeting.

"What would you like to know?"

"Is casting...magic?" His face was without expression and his voice lacked emotion. Bera understood then what Challen had meant by, 'hard to read'.

"Magic is the best human equivalent. Casting has a purpose behind it, but the process is too complex for you and me to grasp. It was originally created for keepers. Not for nephilim and definitely not for humans to understand."

.....

Chapter Thirty-Nine

C hallen kept one eye on Moccasin throughout the journey. He didn't trust him and with good reason. He knew Lawan as a cruel vindictive woman. To his dismay, along the route, Bera uncharacteristically began warming up to the other host so that by the end they were becoming friendly.

Before their arrival at Tavdren's fortress, Bera and Challen, agreed that to manage Lawan, they would need to keep Moccasin under close observation. If Lawan showed any sign of being present, it would be advantageous to notice it immediately. Bera was unclear on what to do if such a circumstance presented itself. Challen tried to act like he had everything under control, although he didn't fool Bera. She figured out that her keeper was just stalling until he could come up with a proper plan.

.....

Bera led Moccasin outside the rear fort gates to the training field. She flopped down beside a log, stretching out her long legs. "You know what your homework was. Let's see if you've practiced."

Moccasin nodded and got into a good stance. He focused his mind and summoned a respectable shield-cast. She could tell that he was struggling with his eyesight. Glasses and an aging were necessary.

"Good."

"Thank ya." He pulled the cast with a confident smile. As the last flicker of the silver cast died, Bera thought she saw hints of maroon flash in his eyes, however, the idea was immediately dismissed. She'd been diligent to the point of paranoia for the two days she'd been his consultant.

With her hands tucked behind her head, Bera leaned against a tree. "Don't get ahead of yourself. You still have a long way to go before being able to withstand a fully strengthened nephilim." She shot out a spear cast to prove her point.

Moccasin sat down next to her. "This

place...what kind of creatures are here?"

The question caught her off guard. "Some from earth and some extinct ones-"

"Extinct?"

"Dodos, Tasmanian Tigers, Irish Elk... some others, I can't think of."

"Really?" Moccasin only knew of the dodo.

"Ya. They can be dangerous, so you want to be careful."

Moccasin dug his heel around in the dirt patch. He was quiet for a moment while Bera watched him, trying to see behind his often-impassive face.

Bera guessed, "That's not really what you really wanted to know."

"Well..." he struggled to find the right words. "What about ghosts? I know that you can also die in this realm, but what then? Is it possible for a nephilim to become a phantom here in Hazdrim?"

"No one knows." Bera shrugged. "There are theories. They say there could be yet another realm. Or we could just be trapped in an endless loop of reliving our deaths. But who cares, right? It's not important."

"Not important?"

"No. Initiation is important."

"I should keep practicin'."

"Yes, you should." Bera got to her feet and prodded his thigh with her boot. "Your DNA results will be coming in a day or two. Be prepared for it."

"Why should I be prepared?"

Bera regretted mentioning the results. "You never know what might surface. For instance, in my results, I learned that I am a closer descendent to Odin than I thought."

"Odin? The Norse god?"

"Yes. The non-human part of me...is my Odin-genes."

Moccasin was perplexed. "I thought the nephilim gene was the non-human part?"

"Ya, nephilim genes. Mine come from Odin." He flinched as Bera whacked him. "Don't correct your superior!"

Moccasin squinted hard at her as she turned to leave.

What is he thinking?

She wasn't sure what to make of Moccasin's line of questions. Although, Challen didn't seem concerned as he walked beside her up the path. He was calm but thoughtful. Thus far, Moccasin appeared to be unaware of his host status.

Don't Moccasin's questions make him nervous?

Challen isn't telling me everything.

.....

She read the DNA results to Challen, and their suspicions were confirmed. Moccasin did have the magus gene, but it would be impossible for him to learn the magus spells. After Nilaon Alleari's suicide, the magus spell books, The Scripts, were destroyed. The only known magus in Tavdren, a hex, was imprisoned and awaiting execution for the murder.

"What do we do?"

Challen stared at the result. *"About Lawan? Or her host?"*

"Both. I think that we need to contact Sundra's host. She might know how to help us deal with this magus. Or I could eliminate him. That approach hasn't failed me. Ever."

"No," Challen shook his head. *"Bera, you know, we need him alive."*

"A quick snap to the neck while he's sleeping." she dusted her hands. "That sounds like a solid plan. No?"

"We have gone over this before. I need them both alive. No killing. Understand?"

Bera reluctantly nodded.

"Sundra was a very sweet girl," Challen explained, *"but not someone who could handle a crisis. She was Lawan's defender. They were like sisters. Until...Lawan turned."*

"Are you saying that she can't be trusted?"

"No. Everyone loves her. And in the end, she joined us to do what was necessary...to take care of Lawan." He slumped against the wall. *"I only worry that she will be reluctant to take action. How would we know where to send the message anyway? I can tell who the hosts are when I see them. But not from a distance. Tell Jin you're unwell and ask her to explain the results to Moccasin. That will give Moccasin have time to consider the results and will give*

us a day to come up with a plan."

"To be fair I did come up with a plan." Bera made neck-snapping motions with her hands. "That easy."

.....

"Everyone looks at me differently. I hate it. They all think I'm a loose cannon that at any moment will explode." Moccasin sat in a chair in the library. It was the only place to have a quiet, unobserved conversation. Not many Tavdren soldiers were avid readers.

Bera was sitting next to him, one leg was thrown over the arm of her chair. She flipped through pages in a book, looking for illustrations. "Good. That means you can prove them wrong." She closed the book, disappointed in the lack of pictures. "Criticism is a good thing."

"It doesn' feel like a good thing."

Bera rolled her eyes. She smacked him with the book.

"Ow!"

She smacked him again. "Stop complaining. Your initiation is coming up fast. You need to stay focused on what's at hand. Don't slip into self-pity."

Moccasin took a deep breath. "I needed that."

Bera smacked him again.

"What was that for?"

"You flinch. It's amusing."

Moccasin snatched a thin book off a

nearby shelf and threw it at her. Bera caught it in mid-air and prepared to hurl it back when a steward peeked his head from around the corner and scolded them.

"You two! Out!"

Bera gently punched Moccasin's shoulder. "Feeling better? Pain is the best way to calm nerves." She tossed the book over her head. A sharp yelp from the steward alerted her that the book had hit its mark. She grinned. "Ready for your aging?"

"I guess." He scratched his ear. "What will it feel like? Will it hurt?"

"It won't hurt me at all."

"I meant me...never mind."

.....

Bera cracked her knuckles and left Moccasin to begin the initiation. She hurried to find her seat in the gallery next to the other consultants.

Challen had strongly disagreed with the aging spell for Moccasin. It proved to make him stronger, and that would either help them or be their doom. He didn't like taking the risk. There was a grave fear of Lawan that wouldn't leave Challen. Any advantage for Moccasin further frustrated his nerves.

Seeing her keeper paranoid annoyed Bera. The more time she'd spent with Moccasin, the more she grew to like him as a nephilim. Challen didn't approve of this growing friendship and cautioned her against getting too close. As Moccasin hadn't shown any signs of having his keeper dominant, it was difficult for Bera to imagine him as a threat.

"Think he'll pass the initiation?"

"Of course! I trained him after all." She weaved through tight rows of chairs.

"But he's paired with the hex who killed Alleari-"

"-He'll be fine."

Challen worried, "He mustn't fail."

"He won't." Atticus had personally requested that he be paired with the hex and Bera approved. As nilaon, Atticus was terrified of the hex and felt only another magus would be able to defeat her. But Bera just wanted to know if he'd actually see it through. To see if he'd kill his own kind.

She reached the front row of the darkened gallery that overlooked the great hall for the initiations. The viewing was an event much looked forward to in all Tavdren, so many were already filing in and finding seats. It didn't take long to find her place with the other highrindh. And it wasn't long for Moccasin to enter the darkened arena. Bera heard Challen catch his breath for a long second then slowly release.

"How can you be so calm?"

"He'll do well." She shrugged and placed one last bet with a nearby soldier. Most were in favor of Moccasin.

Moccasin's silver cast illuminated his face

in the darkness and alerted everyone to his location. Using his cast as a guide, he moved forward into the vast space. He found the cages quickly, and to Bera's great amazement he began a low conversation with the hex. She, and everyone else in the gallery, instinctively leaned in to hear better but was unable to decipher what the two magus were discussing in the battle arena.

Bera could feel the eyes on her, eyes wondering how she'd react to her trainee being such a disappointment. This wasn't the combat they'd anticipated. Some with bets against were premature with their glee. She could hear their sniggering.

After an embarrassingly amount of time, Moccasin stepped up to the cage. Per Atticus' orders, the hex had been bound and stitched with cotton. The two weaknesses of a magus. No one wanted a hex set loose in the fort even for combat. But the truth was, they all knew the hex's real power lay in her mind, not in her physical strength.

It was evident from the silent conversation between the two combatants that the hex was using her magus powers in defense. Bera watched as Moccasin opened the cage. And then it was over. It was a swift and efficient decapitation. The whispered conversation was cut short by one swift motion of the cast sword. Then Moccasin simply extinguished his cast and exited the arena.

Raising her hand to her own neck, Bera was slightly unnerved to see the hex suffer the same death fate as herself. The feeling didn't last as she promptly and quite happily collected her winnings.

"Such bad losers," she cackled with glee at the sour faces.

Stuffing the money in her shirt, she shouldered her way through the bustling crowd. Despite her victory, her gut and Challen's mumblings in her ear were telling her that something was not right with that conversation between the two combatants. She needed to get to Moccasin.

By the time she got to the arena exit, Moccasin was gone. The hex's body was being carted out for burial.

He killed her efficiently.

While examining the clean wound, she heard someone approaching and swung around to see Jin.

"Congratulations, Bera" Jin said coolly, as she walked past her former trainee. "He did well."

Bera raised her chin and lifted her arm, blocking Jin's path. "I have an assignment for you. See if this," she pointed her boot into the body lying on the cart at her feet. "Or Moccasin has had any access to the magus spells."

Jin's familiar malicious smile returned. "Atticus has assured us all that The Script has been destroyed."

"And you and I both know that isn't necessarily the truth." Bera replied. "Why don't you
run along and double-check with your sweetheart."

Jin's face drained of color as she turned on
her heels.

"Told you so," Challen grumbled. *"I did
warn you this could be dangerous."*

Raising a finger to his lips, she mouthed,
"I have enough to do. Shut up."

"You'll see," he groaned. *"That was Lawan,
out there."*

For the first time in a long while, Bera
began to have doubts. She worried about her abilities and strength to keep everything in her control.

.....

Chapter Forty

Bera sat on the cold ground in the training pen. She needed to sort through her thoughts from the recent events. While she lounged against a crate, the Tasmanian Tigers danced around her. She grappled and tousled with the dog-like creatures, enjoying their wet noses and happy licks.

The marsupials were referred to as dogs because their appearance and behavior so closely resembled canines.

"I'm a cat person." Challen curled his nose and shuddered as one of the tigers ran through his translucent figure. *"Has Jin found anything*

about the magus spells? Anything about what they spoke about?"

"I'm meeting with her later." She scratched one of the dogs behind its ear. "We just need confirmation that all the spells are gone."

The keeper sighed and shook his head. *"Was Jin the best nephilim for the job? She has reasons to betray you."*

Bera continued petting the creature in her lap. "You know she was close to Alleari. The very thought of a magus sends her into a fury. Besides, we know that Jin confronted Moccasin after she'd told him his ancestry results. So, he won't be suspicious if Jin tries to force the magus spells secret from him. If the Hex did share a secret with him at all. Jin can get it out of him without me being compromised." The Tasmanian Tiger rolled onto his back for a belly rub. "You admitted that I was right to befriend him, so let Jin do the dirty work."

Challen lifted an eyebrow. *"That's...surprisingly nuanced."* He pushed his curly hair back.

She stopped rubbing the tiger pup. "Thanks." Her fingers took a treat from the bin and tossed it into an open cage. When the marsupial ran inside after it, she latched the gate.

"Bera." Moccasin came through the training center where she was kneeling next to the cages.

"How is life as a new Tavdren soldier treating you?" Bera asked over her shoulder, securing the crate's latch.

"Tiring." He sighed.

Bera saw his silver eyes flash, and for that brief second, his pupils appeared goat-like. She was no expert on the magus. However, she'd learned enough about their kind in the days since discovering Moccasin's magus bloodline, to know that their pupils turn horizontal while attempting a magus spell.

He is practicing spells on me!
He has the spells!
How?

It might be simply an effect of having the gene. Bera couldn't be sure, however, it heightened her concern. If Moccasin was experimenting with his magus traits, she would need to be even more diligent.

"Got something on your mind?" She asked, trying to read his impassive face. Trying to watch his pupils without it being obvious.

Moccasin shook his head. "It was a hard nigh'."

"Why is that?"

Moccasin took a while to respond. "Bad dreams."

"*That's a lie,*" Challen whispered, suddenly appearing at her other side.

"You know, dreams are just extensions of thoughts. Whatever's bothering you needs to be cleared from your thoughts, before it can be cleared from your dreams."

"What? Where'd you get that from?" Moccasin smirked.

"Oh, I read it somewhere." Bera rolled her eyes. She used her axe handle to scratch her back. Both simultaneously erupted in laughter at the idea of her reading. Bera smacked his thigh with the blunt side of her axe.

"Sorry." Moccasin teased in between laughs.

"This is why I don't give advice." Bera stood and walked to the exit. "I'm done helping you."

"I said sorry." Moccasin mocked.

"You really sound sincere, too." Bera pet one of the tigers between the ears. Then turning to Moccasin, she added, "You really should take my advice. Clear your head."

Bera left the kennel with Challen closely following. As they took the path through a cluster of birch trees, they spooked an Irish Elk. It bolted across the worn dirt path and passed right through Challen.

Challen gasped. *"I will never get used to that."* He smoothed down his rumpled black and white shirt.

They watched the beautiful elk disappear into the thicket. The forest around the fort was full of elk which supplied the citizens with a steady supply of meat.

Bera went over the day's plan in her head. She needed a full report from Jin and would then make a sweep of Moccasin's rooms while he was on duty in the stables. The last item on her list was to have a follow-up conversation with Atticus about Moccasin's position at the fort. She intended to convince Atticus that Moccasin's mage status could be useful to him. The nilaon wanted to keep the mage contained where he couldn't do any damage, however, that was a conflict of interest for Bera. She felt the need to once again remind Atticus who was really in charge and that her word was final on the matter. She and she alone would manage Moccasin.

Challen's whining brought her swiftly back to her surroundings.

"...so, then I woke up to find it nibbling one of my toes. Well, you can imagine how I screamed."

"Challen, I don't mean to interrupt, but I could use some quiet. Do you mind flying off somewhere?"

"I don't fly-" Challen started. "Oh, alright." He sighed and then faded out of sight, going into a short hibernation.

Bera had much to do with spinning Atticus and Jin and managing Moccasin to worry with Challen's daily moaning. He was a bored deity trapped with her until his peers arrived. It was the first time that she'd stopped to take it all in. The daily chaos. For centuries now, she'd accepted the idea of being selected by Challen. It made her feel honored and significant. A god-like being needed her help to achieve the supernatural. However, at that very moment, it felt like a curse.

How do I even know that Challen is real?
Maybe he's just my imagination?

Bera had asked herself these questions repeatedly over the years. But evidence for this weak theory was little to none. Challen had proven himself to be reliable in the past. He was a trustworthy source of information around the fort. As long as she was within a certain distance, he could go unseen into any room and observe conversations. This was a primary reason why she had Atticus and the other two highrindh at her command.

She ran the fortress, and no one knew. No one would ever know.

"Bera!" Atticus' voice broke through the quiet.

She smiled and turned in his direction. "How may I assist you, Nilaon?"

"Highrindh Chione from Drundra is expected today. I would like you to personally greet her when she arrives."

"Of course," she replied, nodding. "And I would like a private word with you about Moccasin."

Their eyes met as they assessed each other. The relationship had a public face and a very different private face. They both knew the arrangement.

Atticus replied, "Afterwards." Then he

quickly left her.

Highrindh Chione, being one of the oldest nephilim in the realm, had a reputation of power and great knowledge. Her strategic mind had made her into Drundra's most favored political figure, and it was more than a rumor that she was in line to be Drundra's next nilaon.

Bera was exasperated with this new development. Meeting Chione was an unwelcome twist in her day. A visiting dignitary would complicate matters.

"Challen." She whispered to herself, but there was no response. He was most certainly pouting somewhere in his funny hibernation space. She then remembered instructions on how to summon him, yet there had never been a need until now.

Something about writing his name in blood.
Should have written it down.

.....

Bera waited outside of the main entrance. She'd hand-picked a guard, and they were waiting in full dress armor for their guest's arrival.

There wasn't a long wait before Moccasin came up from the stable yard escorting Chione and her guards to the rear entrance.

To Bera's amazement, the renowned highrindh was small in stature. She was dressed in full battle-ready armor and her face was painted in the Drundran style, so that Bera was unable to make out much of her appearance other than her petite frame. Her casting color was navy as was her attire. What stood out more than all this, however, was how Chione walked. Every single step was with grace and strength.

Her fighting style probably relies on speed and stealth.

Eh, I think I could take her.

After an initial curt exchange, Chione was escorted to her chambers. Awaiting her there was a meal and means of washing. She was then given instructions on when she would be summoned for her meeting with Nilaon Atticus.

It was made clear by the honored guest, that being deposited in her chambers wasn't up to standard, but Bera had other matters to attend to. She couldn't spend much time tending to Highrindh Chione.

Bera's boots clicked against the stone floors, echoing along the halls as she searched for Jin. Challen reappeared, yawning.

"Enjoy your hibernation nap?"

Challen smiled and stretched himself. *"It was a nice break, thanks."* His smile changed into a curious expression. *"Why is Sundra's host here?"*

Bera abruptly halted. "Say what, now?"

Challen explained, *"Sundra is here. Who's this guest?"*

"That's not pos-," Her eyes widened. "Highrindh Chione..."

Challen was excited. *"Thank goodness! I've missed Sundra so much! Let's go back and see her now."*

"Uh, no." Bera snapped. "I currently have another keeper to deal with. You know, Lawan?"

"Well, Lawan-"

Bera tightened her braid. "I need to contain the magus situation. That is the priority. No?"

Challen argued, *"Yes, but-"*

"I'm going to find Jin."

Challen floated in front of her, hands out blocking her path. *"That can wait! We have a rare opportunity to deal with a keeper who isn't a complete nightmare! A keeper who actually likes me and will help us. We'll have to meet up with them eventually because you can bet, Sundra has already told Chione about you!"*

"What happened to..." Bera cleared her throat and did a very bad impression of Challen's voice. "...we must wait for all the others."

"First, I don't sound like that. Second-"

"Yes, you do."

"Second, this is different. Her keeper, Sundra, is my dear friend."

"No."

"Please."

Bera rubbed her forehead. "Fine. But you owe me. That means no complaining for at least a week."

"Deal!" Challen beamed. Not often did he get his way.

They returned to the guest suites in the

south wing of the fort. They rarely had guests because only foreign delegates were brave enough to venture into the Tavdren soldier base. The two approached the door to Chione's suite. Bera prepared to knock, but as she raised her fist, the door was yanked open sending Bera tripping inside.

"Who the-" Bera sputtered, caught off guard.

The visitor growled, "I am not waiting here. Take me to Atticus, now."

Having the advantage, Chione attempted to shove Bera to the ground. Bera was quick and instinctively spun, charging her opponent in one fluid motion. The two highrindh squared off, each making casts that clashed in mid-air.

"*Stop!*" Challen shouted.

Bera rolled her eyes and reabsorbed the cast. Chione was not nearly as polite about the matter. She swiftly advanced, aiming her cast at Bera's throat.

As much as instinct told her to swing back and sidekick Chione in the chest, Bera restrained herself.

Not a nightmare, he said.
Sundra is nice, he said.

Just as suddenly, Chione straightened and pulled the cast away. "Is he here?"

"Who?"

"Don't play games with me. I know you are Challen's host. Now, is that pathetic excuse of a Lawan host with you as well?"

Challen looked Chione up and down. *"Yup. That's her."*

Chione was short but very strong. But her bright blue eyes were intense enough to intimidate anyone into submission. Drundran war paint adorned her cheeks contrasting with her black/navy hair.

"Lawan's host is here in this fortress. And best you guard your tongue. You are in my house." Bera made a shield-cast. "I don't roll over easily."

Chione narrowed her eyes and stared at Bera for a few seconds. "So... you're Challen's host? Sundra was right?"

Bera replied, "Highrindh Bera Aze. And you are Highrindh Chione, the host of Sundra?"

Chione only responded with a crisp nod. She gestured to the table and pulled out a chair. "It appears we have much to discuss."

Bera sat against the wall. "Is Sundra...here?"

"Yes." She pointed to the corner. "And she is very eager to go home. But alas, three of the other hosts have yet to arrive."

"And we can't know when?"

"No." Chione lifted an eyebrow. "Has the Lawan host shown any signs of alignment with Lawan?"

Bera responded, "I don't think he yet knows."

"That's to our advantage."

"There is one problem. He is a mage."

Chione crossed her arms and frowned at Bera. "Well, this isn't good." She was strangely calm. "It really is the worst possible outcome."

"So Challen keeps reminding me." Bera shrugged, "But the most I can do under these circumstances is control where he goes and what he does."

"Does he have the spells?"

"I was in the process of finding this out when you arrived." Bera cast Challen a scathing glance.

The two hosts discussed possible scenarios. They and their keepers had many questions and suggestions on how to proceed with Lawan. It was agreed that Moccasin should be carefully managed, but the task was primarily left to Bera. The specifics were debated well into the afternoon when the guards came to escort Chione to her meeting with Atticus.

.....

Chapter Forty-One

"What do you mean? How can Jin just...leave?" Dulveron asked.

Atticus had called for a meeting with the highrindh and Chione. The room was tense with the news that Jin was gone. She'd been missing for two days, and rumors were circulating among the soldiers and staff. "She's left...without a trace, but you may read the letter she left, if you wish." Atticus stated, placing the paper on his desk.

Bera paced back and forth in front of the closed door. She was replaying in her mind what she'd seen in the barn. Moccasin and Jin had been in a heated argument which unfortunately had escalated to the point of violence.

Jin had threatened and then attacked Moccasin, and in return, he'd stabbed her with a pitchfork. It was a swift and violent act reminiscent of his initiation. Happening so quickly, Bera could hardly believe it when she'd seen it from her hidden position.

It was a quick kill.

Jin had it coming.

Challen had been hibernating at that time. Her keeper assumed Lawan had taken full control. Challen believed Lawan was growing stronger in Moccasin every day. Bera wouldn't accept that it was Lawan because of his reaction afterward. It was pure panic. From what Bera knew of Lawan, she wouldn't have cared enough to panic, much less clean up evidence and bury the body.

Either way, Bera had no intention of speaking out against Moccasin. Jin's death was a frustrating inconvenience for Bera because Jin hadn't found any information on the magus spells. Jin's highrindh position would need filling, and she'd spent centuries cultivating control over Jin that was useful to her ambitions. Bera hated losing that.

And to complicate matters, Chione was still skulking around the fort having private meetings with Atticus. News of a highrindh's murder carried back with Chione would spread to other regions, weakening Tavdren's reputation. Bera's head was spinning on crisis management.

This whole thing is a mess for me.

I'd like to get my hands on him.

The worst part, it was Bera herself who'd sent Jin after Moccasin. To get confirmation about the magus spells. Jin was instructed to goad him into using a magus spell on her, but she went too far off script and the situation blew up. Jin wasn't told to go to the barn. She was to confront him after the initiation, but she'd waited too long.

Aha!

She did this to herself.

Bera's conscience was clear.

But Bera made a note. This would be the last time she would cover for Moccasin. He was becoming increasingly unpredictable and that was a problem for her.

Challen paced at her side once again spinning worrisome threads. *"He gave Lawan control! And she killed Jin!"*

Bera had to keep a straight face in front of the others. She glanced to Atticus who sat solemn at his desk. Across the room, Chione met her gaze and held it.

She's suspicious.

It embarrassed Bera how horribly Atticus was taking the loss of Jin. It was obvious to anyone that his grief was more than that of losing a valued highrindh. He was clearly grieving a lover. She hoped he could get control of himself so no one would put their relationship together. She needed to maintain her hold on Atticus and with Jin gone, her threat over him was moot.

Chione obviously is working it out in her scheming brain.

She's a notorious strategist for a reason.

Which is why, when the nilaon showed her that Jin's notam had vanished from his forearm, Bera convinced Atticus not to reveal it to anyone else. It was pointless to suggest that Jin had simply died of natural causes or by any accident as this would have happened in or around the fortress. It would've been noticed. The only reasonable conclusion for Atticus was that she had been murdered.

Despite his despair, he understood that the murder of his hindringh spilling into the other regions would reflect poorly on him and Tavdren. Especially after his predecessor had been murdered by a hex. One fleeing highrindh was bad enough; a murder would raise unwanted questions.

Tavdren must maintain its reputation of strength and unity.

Bera couldn't imagine the kind of trouble Moccasin's mess would lead to if Atticus discovered he'd killed Jin. The nilaon was fervently searching for any excuse to execute the mage and certainly wouldn't hesitate over the murder of his highrindh. His lover.

Bera needed to tread very carefully in these uncertain waters. It benefited her and the nilaon to keep everyone believing Jin had fled. It benefited Tavdren for Chione to return home never knowing a highrindh had been murdered. And that is why Bera had written the letter. In it she had Jin write of falling in love and wanting a family, something forbidden to highrindh.

"Should we send out search parties?" She asked.

"No" Atticus sighed. "If she comes back to Tavdren territory, tradition states that she is it be executed on the spot."

"This is just a great day for you, isn't it?"

Bera couldn't resist rolling her eyes at Challen.

Atticus took offense at this, believing she'd meant it for him. "You find this amusing, Bera?"

"No, Sir." She scrambled to find a good excuse. "The old rules are outdated and could be amended. Jin wrote of her personal reasons for leaving. It's not wrong to want to have a family. Surely you agree."

"The law is the law." Dulveron objected.

"Of course. Laws must not be broken." Bera looked Atticus dead in the eyes and let the words fall upon the quiet room. Only he knew what the warning implied.

Atticus took it correctly, changing the

subject. "Then there's the matter of choosing a new highrindh."

Chione glanced knowingly from Atticus then back to Bera. Bera regretted putting too much on display for the nosey foreigner.

She heard Challen snickering again. The keeper enjoyed a good show.

"What about Kodry as the highrindh?" Dulveron suggested.

Bera shook her head. "Kodry is short-tempered and stubborn. We need someone more flexible. Willing to hear all sides. And find logical solutions. We shouldn't rush into this decision."

.....

Atticus hadn't requested search patrols because he feared Jin's body being found. But he did want to find Jin, so Bera agreed, under the guise of hunting, to conduct a thorough and discreet search. Of course, she knew exactly where the body had been buried and had no worries of it ever being found. After some time had passed, Bera would simply inform the nilaon that after an extensive search, Jin's body was nowhere to in the area.

The lengths I go to.

Taking advantage of Challen's absence, Bera went up to her rooms and collected her bow. Because she was a member of the hunters that provided the fortress with fresh meat, it was natural for her to use her time in the forest as a hunt.

.....

The sky was cloudless, and the warm sun was on her back as Bera followed deer tracks across the forest floor. The game trail was packed down from years of use. She stayed light on her feet and made sure not to step on any fallen leaves. If she was correct, her prey would be close by. Any sudden movements or sounds would disturb it.

She crouched down and carefully examined a fresh set of tracks. The trail there was thick, but from experience she knew it would open up at the nearby stream. From where she crouched, she could hear the water.

Bera followed the trail toward the edge of a creek, and from the opposite bank, she heard the animal drinking. The brush was providing her cover so that she wouldn't spook her target. Slowing her breathing, she waited to gently maneuver her body into a shooting position.

Bera drew her bow back and bent her knees. Remaining as quiet as a dove, she crept forward and around a tree preparing her shot. Her fingers tightened around the bow, but then she gently lowered it. This was no deer.

Standing directly across from her on the other bank was a large grey wolf. It had striking yellow eyes that stared back at her. Water dripped from its chin and onto its white underbelly which was stained with the blood of recent prey.

"Ah." Bera took two steps backward. "I see

this was your deer. I am lucky that you are nice and full, huh?"

The wolf turned its head to the side in a questioning manner. Its eyes blinked slowly as if it was thinking through whether or not to charge at Bera.

"I will leave you to your drink, then," Bera said, careful not to show her teeth. She eased her bow down to her side.

She didn't turn her back on the wolf until it disappeared into the underbrush on the opposite side of the stream. Bera took a deep, steadying breath and decided to return to the fort.

Where was its pack?

.....

Bera approached the fort's rear entrance and rolled her shoulders and neck. The incident with the wolf had jarred her nerves. She was fortunate that it had eaten its supper and even more so that it was alone. Finding a wolf without its pack was unusual, and she knew that she wouldn't have survived against a hungry pack.

As Bera began to step onto the gravel path, she heard a movement from the edge of the forest. She slowly turned her head in the direction. And there it was again. Sitting on its haunches just past the tree line was the grey wolf. The sun filtered through the leaves leaving patches of shadow on its thick fur coat. The wolf had followed her.

"Hello, again." Bera nodded, giving the

regal animal proper respect.

The wolf flopped its large tail from side to side and Bera would have sworn that the wolf curled the corners of its lips into a canine grin.

Bera smiled in return, still without showing any teeth. "You are very beautiful."

It then surprised Bera, when it stood up and trotted over to her. It sat at her heels.

"Oh, my." Bera was completely still. They looked at each other for a long moment. When Bera felt confident, she carefully extended her palm for the animal to learn her scent.

The wolf sniffed her hand and up her arm. Then it began to rub its head against Bera's hands and made a soft shuffle sound. *You are mine now.* She seemed to say.

Bera, having little to no clue as to how to handle the situation, softly pet its head. "You are very soft, sweet girl." For she had determined that the magnificent beast was indeed a female. "It was pleasant meeting you, but I'm afraid I must return to my duties."

The grey wolf rubbed past Bera and pawed at the fort's door.

"I guess you are coming in then." Bera wasn't one to question this sign from Odin. Wolves were special.

She opened the door for the wolf and waited to see where it would go. The wolf padded into the building and stopped not far from the threshold. It appeared to be waiting for Bera.

"Do you want to see my home? It's down this hall and up a flight of stairs." She gestured for the canine to follow her. And to her continued amazement, it did.

Bera and her new friend walked to the stairs and up to her corridor. They received a few curious glances from busy soldiers passing by, but all knew better than to question the intentions of Highrindh Bera.

The grey wolf was led into Bera's room and didn't waste time finding the softest spot on Bera's rug to lay down. It looked up to her expectantly.

"Make yourself at home." Bera shrugged.

Challen appeared next to her. *"Is that a wolf?"*

"Yes." she put her hands on her hips and smiled at her canine companion. "Vali. She is called Vali."

.....

Part Five

.....

Chapter Forty-Two

Bera was leading another group of Wakers through the Tavdren birch forest. The path was well known to her by now, making these journeys was something she looked forward to.

Her memories from earth were faint now, and her life as a Tavdren highrindh was all she knew. One day, very long ago, she hadn't been able to picture her brother's face. It was all gone. Only his name and the sound of his voice stayed firmly implanted in her soul. But Bera had learned to push those thoughts aside and to keep her chin up. Survival depended on the appearance of strength. She was a Tavdren highrindh. No longer a Viking shieldmaiden.

The Wakers that stood apart in this new group were two young men, Benjamin Toll and Wift T. Stillwood because Challen immediately and quite excitedly recognized the Wakers as hosts. The younger one, Ben, was Venner's host while Wift was host to Tavious, Tavdren's namesake.

It was extraordinary that the two keepers arrived in the same group.

To Bera's disappointment, both chose to live in Tavdren. The last thing she wanted to take on was more keeper hosts. Managing Moccasin all these years had been enough of a challenge despite their friendship.

Pushing her complaints aside, Bera did understand that having them close was advantageous. It would save her valuable time later, by not having to track them all through the different regions.

The greater concern was the meeting between Wift and Moccasin. Challen had explained to her that Lawan and Tavious were bitter enemies. He'd warned her that their rivalry would have certainly been passed on to their host Wakers. And he fully expected Lawan to come forth at the arrival of her arch enemy.

Ben was talkative. The Waker was chatty to the point where one wondered if there was anything he wouldn't turn into a rambling conversation. He was buoyant and friendly. Bera wanted to dislike him, but he was obedient and listened carefully to all she had to say. And because of this, his cheery disposition slowly grew on her.

He didn't strike Bera as a keeper's host at all. If his keeper had made herself known, Ben didn't show it in his behavior.

Ben was slim and of average height, with black skin and a contagious, broad smile. His casting color was likely light purple per his violet eyes.

The other host, Wift, soon revealed himself to be a potential problem. Along the way, he'd made snap decisions and was free with his opinions, not unlike Moccasin in the beginning. These were very bad traits if she was ever going to keep all the hosts in her region docile. Most significantly, Tavdren didn't tolerate such insolence from recruits. She predicted he wouldn't fare well at the fort.

Wift was a bit smaller in stature than Ben but made up for it in muscle. He had pale skin, dark hair, and green eyes. Something was oddly familiar in his features and mannerisms, although she couldn't connect her thoughts as to how or why.

A thought hovered on the edges of her mind, teasing her with what the connection could be, but it remained elusive.

Challen walked next to Bera at the head

of the group, nearly skipping with excitement. *"That means only one host is left to arrive. Golovar."*

"He better not come here." She kicked a rock. "I am getting tired of babysitting hosts."

"Remember, we need the keepers all together eventually." he shook his curly head. *"Plus, you've managed Moccasin just fine."*

Atticus had promoted Moccasin to the position of highrindh after Dulveron died in battle. It really hadn't been Atticus' decision. Bera had found that with the right amount of his favorite beverage, Moccasin was easily controllable. In her estimation that made him the safest choice to fill the position. It also kept him close so she could monitor the level of Lawan's influence.

With Bera's prompting, and because he was fiercely loyal, Moccasin had gained Atticus' trust.

Many years ago, during an evening of excessive inebriation, she'd discovered his access to the magus script. The signs had been there all along. Bera had gotten him drinking and coerced a confession out of him, and the next day she'd confronted him. She realized his gift could be used to her advantage. Having a feared yet controllable magus highrindh under her thumb was ideal for Bera. It was even better that they'd become friends. Theirs wasn't a rivalry like the relationship she had with Jin.

Atticus had been difficult to talk down from executing Moccasin when she'd told him about the still existing magus script and his proficiency with the spells. Bera still maintained a firm hand on Atticus, and he was soon made to realize how beneficial Moccasin could be to them all. Time and testing had been the final confirmation that Moccasin was their mage.

"Bera! How long till we arrive at the castle?" Ben jogged up and asked eagerly.

"Fort," she corrected. "It depends on how many times we stop for breaks."

Ben nodded and looked at the trees as they walked. He would make for a good consultee. He was malleable, but with flashes of raw casting talent. She would likely select him.

"Are all trees in Tavdren birch?" He asked with an abundance of curiosity. "Also do you have phones?"

"Birch here but in the northeast and south there are more varieties." Bera narrowed her eyes. "Phone?"

"Yeah, do you have phones? Things you call people on. What about record players? Or cars?"

Bera smiled and sighed. "Calls? I do not understand this phone." she paused. "You know you are not on earth, correct?"

"Yeah." he nodded.

Bera continued, "And you understand that your people are still alive on earth?"

"Oh sure. The docs at the center explained it to me."

"Then you must know that you are…"

"Dead? Yes, but I feel so alive." He grinned at her. "You know something? I'm really diggin' this place."

"I think I know what you mean, but you may not feel this way when we get to Tavdren." Bera laughed, "You are a funny one, aren't you?"

"That's what I've been told!"

She turned to do a headcount and Ben slowed a bit to speak with Wift. She would need to keep her eyes on the two of them, especially when they were together.

…..

The last group of Wakers separated from her and the fort recruits. They were nearing the small village a few miles from the fort. To her surprise, Atticus was waiting for her on a dirt road on the outskirts.

He sat mounted upon his massive shire steed, Caesar, and beckoned her. "Bera, I must speak with you."

She was suspicious because the nilaon should never leave the fort without an escort. Tightening her red braids, she left the others and approached her commander. "Of course, Sir."

Atticus dismounted smoothly and taking Bera's by the arm, he pulled her to the side.

She was concerned at the manic look in his eyes. Atticus hadn't been this disturbed since Jin's *disappearance.* She started to speculate on possible emergencies while he gathered his words. He was nervous about something. "What's wrong?"

He cast his eyes over her shoulder to the waiting recruits. "It's about Jin."

"What's happened?" Bera lifted an eyebrow. "You didn't find her...did you?"

"No." Again, he looked to make sure no one was listening. "You are aware that time in our realm is different from earthly time?"

"Of course." Bera wished he would get on with it. Atticus had an annoying habit of beating circles around a point.

"There was a time when Jin went on a long mission."

"Mm-hmm." she nodded.

Atticus continued glancing behind her. "But it was more a personal than official mission."

"Yes?" Bera's heart jumped in her chest.

It was clear Atticus was beyond troubled. He could barely speak. "She was...she had a child."

"Mm-hmm." Bera started. "Wait...what?"

"Oh, Dear." Challen popped up at this tasty gossip.

"Jin went to the Waking Facility to have the child and paid a physician to send the child to earth. But the thing is... the time difference made..." He started rambling.

She wanted to slap him. "Hold on-"

"Let him finish!" Challen was on his tip-

toes. *"This is getting good."*

"I've received a message from the physician who performed The Sending. And he says the child..."

Challen leaned in. *"Oh, for goodness' sake."*

"The child has passed through the Waking Center. And is here now." He pointed a shaking finger at the group of Wakers behind them.

Without turning, Bera knew immediately who it was. She'd recognized the familiarity in that Waker from the very beginning of the journey, although it had haunted her as to the significance. It was Wift T. Stillwood.

"Ah!" Challen sighed. *"It all makes sense now, doesn't it?"*

"No. It doesn't," she mumbled under her breath so Atticus wouldn't hear.

"I have so many questions!"

Bera turned her attention to Atticus. "Of course, you'll need this kept a secret." she smiled, innocently.

He shook his head. "Wift can't stay in Tavdren. He's too much of a threat to my position. You need to get rid of him, today."

"Mm-hmm."

.....

Chapter Forty-Three

"**H**as Wift driven you crazy, yet?" Moccasin as he pulled the plug from a bottle with his teeth.

Bera fell into her armchair. She watched him pour himself a drink. "No. He's surprisingly quiet." She tilted her head. She didn't want to talk to him about Wift. "Did you get a haircut?"

Moccasin took a long swallow. "I don't like him." he rubbed his forehead.

"Well, that's a shocker," Challen muttered from who knows where.

Being back on Wift made Bera flinch. "Why?"

Moccasin swirled the amber liquid in his glass. "I'm not sure. Something about him rubs me the wrong way. I trust my gut. Like cats. You try to pet them, and they make you bleed! You either love 'em or you hate 'em."

She sighed and rested her head on the arm of the chair. "Maybe you need to take a break."

"A break, huh?" Moccasin grumbled, indicating that he didn't appreciate the comment. "Too much work to do with Ben. Atticus needs these recruits ready for initiation by the weekend."

Bera noticed he'd recently taken to complaining like a petulant teen. This was likely due to his drinking. She watched quietly as he plopped into the chair beside her. For just an instant, eyes flashed to the magus goat-eyes.

"I think if I have to hear one more story about skate-night at the rink, I'm gonna break Ben's jaw," Moccasin grumbled. "Did you know he was raised in a wealthy family?"

"I didn't know that." She stood and tried to take the bottle from him. "Maybe that's enough."

Moccasin clutched the bottle. "I'm fine." *You really aren't.*

"Fine. Keep drinking." She whistled for Vali. Her wolf had gotten along well in the suite and was quite happy following Bera around on her highrindh duties.

Hating that she was unsuccessful the first

time, Bera tried again to take the bottle from him. Moccasin resisted letting it go which led to a tugging match. Competitive instincts were awakened in both.

"Stop it!" Moccasin growled.

Bera hissed, "Let go!" and tugged harder.

It was obvious Moccasin had too much. She walked a fine line between keeping him controllable with the bottle and him getting out of control.

"Fine. You win. I was goin' anyway." Moccasin let go of the bottle, sending Bera stumbling back with the drink spilling out over her arm. She tossed the bottle to the side where it landed near Vali, causing her to snarl.

Well, I did this to myself.

Shouldn't have given him a key to my cabinet.

Reached out to steady him, Bera said. "Let's get you back to your rooms."

"No!" He swatted at her hands.

She leaned to the right, avoiding his sloppy attempt. "That wasn't a suggestion."

Bera maneuvered him by the shoulders out of her suite and steered him down the hallway. She'd made this trek countless times before, over the years. It was amusing to watch him try and find his way. Several times he'd tripped over his own feet.

Moccasin whispered to himself, as he crashed into his door and tried to turn the knob. "It isn't working." he looked back at her helplessly.

"That's because you need a key." she sighed and stared at him blankly. "Moccasin. Where's your key?"

"I have the key."

Fantastic.

This is just getting more and more fun, isn't it?

Patting his pockets, he chuckled, "I do not have the key."

Bera shook her head in exasperation. She knelt down and began picking the lock. This too, she'd done countless times. Over her shoulder, she could hear his incoherent mumblings. Finally, the lock popped, and she sighed with relief. "Sleep well, sweet prince."

"Can I?"

She ignored that and shoved him inside.

Moccasin appeared clueless as to where he was. "This ain't home."

"There. There." she patted his back. "Try not to do anything too stupid."

"Yes, ma'am."

"Don't call me that," she warned, pointing a finger at his face.

Moccasin grabbed her finger and pulled her in closer for a kiss. Bera's eyes widened, and she was frozen in shock for a few long seconds. She didn't know how to react. Then getting a hold of herself and coming to a decision, she roughly elbowed him in the ribs, knocking his glasses off in the process.

Moccasin fell back against the door frame with a confused expression on his face. "Ow!" He rubbed his shoulder. "That hurt."

"Sleep in tomorrow." Bera patted his head, stepped back, and slammed the door. "You'll need it." She yelled from the other side.

Bera found herself slightly amused by the gesture.

It's not so much that he tried, it's that he's drunk.

.....

Wift and Ben were sparring in the training hall because rain was pouring outside the fortress's thick walls. Bera sat watching from the side. Occasionally a jarring crack of lightning flashed from the windows and thunder was heard rolling overhead.

The two were much improved, although Ben wasn't as strong on offense as Wift. Over the centuries and with much difficulty, Bera had learned to read Moccasin somewhat. She now could see that Ben's cautious offensive style bothered Moccasin. It shouldn't have. She'd once believed and taught her consultees not to think but cast on instinct. Now she was more deliberate in her casting approach.

"You don't have to attack outright. Try taking your opponent off guard by absorbing the cast, then shooting a cast back up once they feel comfortable." Moccasin stalked around the ring, shouting advice to the recruits.

He'd turned into a capable highrindh, and

she was noticing that he was a formidable strategist. Unexpectedly she recalled his unsuccessful kiss, and just as quickly she shoved it from her mind. That wasn't the first time it had popped up. Fortunately for her, Moccasin had forgotten all about the incident from the other night.

Ben nodded at the suggestion and attempted the move. Wift used a green shield cast for a block, however, Ben's new trick ended with Wift being pushed back, disoriented.

"Yes! Very good." Moccasin yelled from the side.

Bera agreed with a nod. Then nodded to Wift, "You can counter by advancing heavily on the legs. Try knocking him down."

Wift took her advice and advanced smoothly.

The two highrindh watched them spar until the young men were staggering from exhaustion. As they were cooling down, Moccasin and Bera went over their mistakes and how to correct them.

After recruits had left for the showers and their duties, and Moccasin had gone, Bera was left alone in the empty hall with her thoughts. Her eyes found the slit windows and watched lightning flash. Absently, she practiced some of her own casts. Shield, sword, and staff all glowing red. The most common shapes.

The quiet was punctured by Atticus barking her name. The sound reverberated around the empty stone training hall catching her by surprise. She swung around, whipping her red sword-cast past his throat, and immediately absorbed it. "How may I help you?"

Atticus didn't hide his frustration. "I made it clear, I wanted you to send Stillwood away!"

"Yes. I know, but there has been a change in plans." She returned a sweet smile. Bera could be very disarming when she smiled. She was lovely when she wanted to be.

Atticus took a calming breath. "You must love making my life difficult."

"I am making *my life* comfortable. It matters not how it impacts you." She skipped into the sparring ring. This was an unspoken challenge. Bera cast a battle axe and twirled it tauntingly.

Bera needed Wift in Tavdren so the keepers would be under her careful eye. However, she obviously couldn't divulge this to Atticus. However, there was another reason for Wift being there, and she felt no worry in sharing that one with the nilaon.

"Poor Atticus. Did you think I would pass up an opportunity to keep you in line?" She shrugged. "Huh?"

Atticus was resigned, but not defeated. He sighed "This will come back on you."

He'd made these threats before over countless years. Bera and Atticus both understood that as long as the Nephilim Realm re-garded him as the true Tavdren nilaon, he was stuck.

"You will push too far and stumble. I am waiting for that."

"Mm-Hmm."

…..

Bera petted Vali's stomach. The wolf rolled onto her back and completely leaned into the belly rub.

"Good girl." Bera crooned. Vali gnawed one of her fingers. Bera smiled. "Hungry? Want supper?"

Vali responded with a low growl.

"Use your words."

Vali replied with two high barks.

"I'm taking that as a yes." She laughed.

Bera stood and then nudged Vali with her shoe. "Let's eat, sweet girl." She led the wolf to her bowl. Bera cut several chunks of meat into the dish, and the sound caused Vali to happily stomp her front paws. She jumped beside Bera and dived into her dinner the second Bera set it down.

It was then that she heard a thudding noise coming from the hall, just outside her door. Vali was too distracted by the food to bark at the unusual sound. Bera sighed and went to see what was happening outside her chambers. She whipped the door open with a sharp. "Hello?"

To her surprise, Moccasin was not out there. He had a habit of stopping by at this time for a drink, a meal, or just to complain. Often all three.

No one was there. Bera took a slow step into the hall and looked both ways. Not a soul could be seen or heard. She created a shield-cast. *This is definitely strange.*

Challen appeared over her shoulder and whispered. *"What's going on?"*

The Keeper stepped out of the doorway. He looked up and down then shrugged. Turning around to face her, Challen began to speak then gasped. He pointed to the wall, his eyes wide in shock.

"What is it?" Bera snapped.

"The wall."

She stepped into the hall and turned to face the stone corridor wall. Her eyes widened in disbelief. A set of words written in a red substance dripped down the wall.

The Real Nilaon

"Son of a beiskadli...what now?"

.....

Chapter Forty-Four

"**M**occasin, I swear to the gods!"

"I don't know anything about this!" Moccasin ran his fingers through the substance on her wall. "What do you think it means? Someone maybe thinks you are next in line?"

Bera had stormed into Moccasin's suite and dragged him to her door. Now she was interrogating him on Challen's behalf. The keeper was convinced Lawan was behind the stained words.

"He's lying," the keeper hissed in her ear.

Moccasin rubbed his tired eyes. "Tell me

again what happened?"

She repeated her account leaving no detail out which only worsened her mood.

He stifled a yawn. "Listen, Bera, whoever did this is trying to intimidate you. Perhaps they don't want you to be nilaon. Nothing can be done tonight. Let's worry about this tomorrow."

"Whoever did this is going to lose an eye when I catch them!" Bera hissed. "I will bring Odin's fury down on them!"

"That's the spirit." Moccasin patted her shoulders. "Can I go back to sleep now?"

"Yeah, sure." Bera pushed him out of her doorway. "Go to your bed. Best friends are supposed to support crazy, middle of the night, vengeance schemes."

"I'm supporting you," He yawned, raising his thumbs.

"That's not what supportive looks like."

"Bera, you don't-" The door was slammed shut before Moccasin could finish his sentence.

Bera slumped her tired body against the back of the door. "He knows nothing about this."

"I still think-"

"Moccasin believes Atticus is still in control. You heard him. He thinks this is about me being next in line for nilaon." She rubbed her forehead. "This is someone's way of telling me that they know who's really in charge."

.....

Bera waited impatiently for Wift to arrive.

His initiation was first, and his late arrival was infuriating. She paced the holding room, growing more agitated by the second until finally, Wift thundered in.

"You're late." She growled, as he hurriedly belted and buckled his armor in place.

He gave a small scowl, offering no excuse.

Bera stomped her boot. "This is one of the most important moments of your afterlife!"

Once again, Wift ignored her.

Bera was used to his stubbornness by this time, yet today she was enraged by his lack of concern for the task ahead. She'd never had a consultee fail, although her gut told her that today would be the first.

"Could you leave?" He looked her in the eye. "You're distracting me."

Bera clenched her fists to keep from casting a dagger at his insolence. She watched in stony silence as he continued about his task of getting ready. She wasn't pleased with being challenged in this manner but was wise enough not to jeopardize his initiation with further argument.

When Wift was focused and ready, he turned on his heels without any word to her and followed the guard out of the room.

Bera watched him go. "You only think this is over, fool."

Composing herself, she walked up to the gallery to find her seat beside Highrindh Moccasin and Grace.

·····

The initiations went well. Wift was flaw-less in his casting. He advanced without hesi-tation and kept his opponent on the defensive until the fatal blow. Wift was measured and in complete strategic control throughout the fight.

Ben's however was an erratic parlay. Moc-casin anxiously watched Ben's performance. It was painful to see Ben's reluctance to engage his opponent. Ben's final blow to the prisoner was in self-defense, which no consultant wants to see. Regardless, Bera made a nice winning from all the performances, including Ben's disappointing efforts.

Bera was relieved that Wift hadn't let her down, yet what had her elated was being rid of him. He'd been a menace in her life the last few weeks. She would continue to keep watch on him even though she wouldn't be required to work specifically with him now that his initiation was complete. Now there was no reason to interact with him. This was a pleasant thought.

Bera and Challen took their time as they walked to the celebration. The first half of the party was formal and stiff with toasts and long dull speeches.

Once Atticus leaves, well, that's when the real party begins.

"Highrindh Bera." Ben eased up beside her in the corridor and whispered. "May I speak with you?"

She smiled warmly and turned to him. "Yes. Is something wrong?"

Ben shrugged. "Could be. I can't say for sure."

"What is it?"

"Well, you see..." Ben scratched the top of his head. "...yesterday I couldn't help but notice that Atticus and Wift were talking very seriously for some time. Wift's reaction was hostile. He was really mad. And then I remembered the day when you were first guiding us, Wakers, to the fort...when we first saw Atticus and he seemed very upset... now considering yesterday..."

Challen groaned. *"Oh, no."*

Ben continued, not hearing the keeper's voice. "Something is going on. Wift could be in some trouble." Ben looked around the hall. "If I could guess, I would say that Atticus has some sort of problem with Wift. That Wift's in big trouble."

Bera tried her best to remain calm.

He paused waiting for her to respond. "Don't know what it could be, but I'm sure there is bad joo-joo between them."

"There is no joo-joo. You can take my word on it." She should have remembered that Ben, or Skates as she liked to call him, was very observant. And a bit of an eavesdropper. "It's fine, trust me."

"Oh," Ben looked like he did not believe

315

her. "Okay, cool." But just as he was turning to leave, he spun back to her. "Wait! Let me see your hands."

"Huh?"

"Your fingers." he asked, "You said I could take your word. Are your fingers crossed?"

Bera held her hands up for inspection. "Why would my fingers cross?"

He tilted his head. "That's what I thought. But then, you never know."

"What are you talking about, Skates?"

Ben cleared his throat. "When a person crosses their fingers while making a promise, the action of finger-crossing reverses the promise. It allows you to lie with immunity."

Bera looked at Ben for a quiet moment. "This is some magic?" She asked, confused.

"He is an idiot," Challen muttered.

"No. It's...well yeah, kinda. Sort of like magic, I guess." Ben smiled, "Funny, I never thought of it like magic before."

Bera was amazed and began crossing and uncrossing her fingers. "Witchcraft!" She shoved her fingers in Ben's face. "I can do so much lying with this!"

"Er-" Ben shrugged. "You're welcome. Oh, before I forget," He snapped his fingers, and let another tasty bit of gossip slip. "Wift disappeared last night and came back to his quarters all wound up." Ben whispered, "I thought I heard him talking to someone. But nobody else was there. None that I could see, at least. But I did see he had something in his hand that he was trying to keep hidden...a small bottle."

"Bottle?" Bera's eyes narrowed. "What kind of small bottle?" She was crossing and uncrossing her fingers absentmindedly practicing for future use.

"Dunno. Some tiny vial." Ben shook his head, his eyes nervously moved over the people passing by. "I'm just worried because I saw this movie with my cousin at a drive-in, where a wife poisoned her husband because she'd caught him having an affair."

"What are you saying? You think Atticus and Wift are having an affair?"

Challen sighed, *"Bera, the boy is a nincompoop."*

"No!" Ben looked amused. "What I mean is, do you think Wift has a reason to- ya know..." Ben rolled his hands.

"Have an affair?" She asked. A passing soldier shot her a curious glance, and Bera nodded hello.

"No! Does Wift T. Stillwood have a reason to poison Nilaon Atticus?"

.....

Bera shoved her way through the crowd. She needed to find Wift before he did anything idiotic.

"You better hurry." Challen urged.

"Ya, I know that!"

She still didn't know why the responsibility had fallen onto her. And it didn't. It also fell onto Ben, who was running right beside her trying to keep pace.

"A crime of passion! The oldest story in the book." Ben shouted over the loud chatter. "But something is missing. The motives don't completely add up."

"Skates, not now." Bera spotted Wift ahead, just turning onto hallway where the highrindh suites were located. She sped up, pushing Ben behind a corner. "Stay here."

He nodded, "You bet."

Ben's spying on Atticus and Wift annoyed Bera, but that was the least of her worries. She would deal with it later.

"Wift!" Bera called.

Wift spun at his name and appeared surprised to see her. He greeted her with false innocence in his tone. "Highrindh Bera. Good evening."

"What are you doing in this wing? It's for highrindh."

Wift avoided making eye contact. He stared down the corridor at nothing that could be identified, as if trying to make up his mind.

"Explain yourself!" Bera ordered.

"I suppose I am lost." Wift shrugged and tried to go around her.

Bera raised her arm and blocked his path. "You're going to tell me exactly what you are doing here."

Wift made eye contact then, and she didn't like what she saw. Barely contained fury was on the surface.

"What makes you think I'm doing anything?" He smiled ruefully and stunned her with his next words. "Are you angry about the message on your wall?"

Bera was too surprised by his question to prevent Wift from leaving.

What?

The real nilaon!

Some things are starting to make sense.

Challen tried to grab Bera's attention. *"Bera!"*

Her mind was clouded with indecision.

"Bera!" Challen yelled.

"I have to get to Atticus."

.....

Once in the dining hall, Bera slid into a chair next to Moccasin and Atticus at the high table. She immediately picked up the nearest wine bottle and examined it.

Moccasin glanced at her questioningly when he caught her fingering and smelling the cork. Bera ignored him, staring hard at the nilaon. She was relieved to see that he wasn't drinking his usual wine. If Wift was going to poison Atticus, it would be the wine. "How's everyone doing, tonight?"

Atticus squeezed his eyes shut and took

another sip from his glass. "I'm feeling a bit tired, actually."

A tiny vial.

Waves of panic shot through her. Bera looked pointedly at his glass. It didn't appear to her that Atticus had drunk anything peculiar or was acting differently. It was just pure luck that he was having whiskey. Finding the compromised wine bottle was the most important thing at the moment.

"Going to call it a night?" She asked, trying to sound casual while ignoring Moccasin's stare.

"Nonsense!" Atticus blinked a few times with a glazed face and continued. "The celebration has barely begun."

Bera pretended to be serving herself from the platters of food and starting a light conversation. However, she was scanning the half-empty bottles on the high table.

It could be any one of these!

Anyone at this table could've had some!

Bera froze at that thought and whipped Moccasin around to face her, so she could see if he was showing signs of poison. "Hey, buddy! Whatcha doing, later?"

Moccasin was staring blankly across the hall. "Moc, are you listening?" She asked, trying to detect any side effects.

He sharply turned back to her. "No... sorry. What did you say?"

Immediately Bera ascertained that there

was nothing unusual in his eyes or voice to cause further concern. She breathed a sigh and quickly tried to say something mundane. "I think we should lessen the number of patrols."

"Yeah. Good idea." It was clear that he wasn't really listening. At this point, she didn't care. Her focus was back on the nilaon.

Atticus coughed into his fist and his face was flushed with beads of sweat on his forehead. "I think the whiskey has gotten to me." He shook himself and stood up. "I'm turning in early. Good night."

He left the table and disappeared into the crowd. She watched him, not certain what to think or what to do next. Perhaps the vial meant nothing.

Well, there he goes.

He is in Odin's hands now!

There were only a few bottles left to check.

So far, so good.

Moccasin shut his eyes. "Can I leave now?"

"No." Bera kicked him from under the table.

"Well, in that case…" He reached for the closest bottle.

Bera snatched it from him. There was a twitch in her left eye and a nervous smile plastered on her face. "I'll take that."

"Hey, you said you wanted a drinking buddy!"

"Oh, stop. I'm just trying to help you." Bera could feel her eye jerk compulsively. She held the bottle close and sniffed the contents. It was distinctly off. A tad sweeter smelling than it should be.

"Strange," she muttered to herself.

Moccasin pointed at her eye, "Yeah, what's going on with you? You're actin' weird."

"The whiskey smells...off."

Moccasin scooted in closer and reached for the bottle. "What do you mean?"

Bera pulled the bottle to her nose and sniffed it again. "Who drank from this?"
Sanguis posion.

Challen noticed her strange reaction. *"Why would Wift poison the whiskey? Atticus usually drinks wine."*

Moccasin's response was her worst nightmare. "Atticus was the only one here before I came in." His eyes widened. "Wait, give me the bottle."

.....

It all happened so quickly Bera couldn't remember all the details even when asked about it the very next day. It was a frenzy of activity leading up to the discovery of Atticus' dead body and the chaos that ensued.

With what Challen could piece together, combined with everything Ben had told her, Bera was certain Wift had known Atticus was his father. And he knew that his parents had sent him away to earth as an infant. Wift continued to deny any involvement in Atticus' murder, although he had a motive. Bera had seen the rage in his eyes in the corridor. She knew he was capable of committing the crime, and he'd had the opportunity.

The whiskey had been compromised earlier in the day, which must have been why Wift was late to his initiation. Bera remembered how cool and distant he was when he'd finally arrived to dress for the battle. He had offered no excuse for his tardiness.

Bera suspected that Wift's keeper was behind this, causing mayhem for his host. In her mind, it explained how Wift could've known about his parentage from his Waking. The keeper, Tavious, must have told him.

The highrindh had several tense meetings on how to inform the fort that Nilaon Atticus had passed. There was a disagreement on what exactly would be said. Details of his death would soon spread to all the regions, and the highrindh couldn't risk Tavdren looking weak.

Throughout all of this, Moccasin was a wreck in front of his peers. He repeatedly claimed that because the poison was in the whiskey, it must've been intended for him. Bera knew it was not, although she couldn't explain her reasons why. Even though she didn't like the turn Moccasin was taking, the truth would have to wait.

If it did come out that he killed his father, Nilaon Atticus, Wift would be executed. Bera and Challen couldn't let that happen because he was still Tavious' host. It required all of her willpower for Bera to resist the urge to turn Wift in, but her revenge could wait. She found him in the training hall by himself.

"Wift, we need to talk." Bera's voice carried in the empty hall. She hopped into the ring and walked casually up to him. And then, without warning or any hesitation, she grabbed his left hand and twisted it behind his back, pushing it up with enough force to draw a sharp gasp.

"Let's go someplace, quiet." she hissed in his ear, pushing him out of the arena. "Where no one can hear your screams."

Wift struggled against her, but she was quick to slam her free fist into the side of his head.

"Be still," she ordered, shoving him into a storage room where she spun him to face her.

"What the hell were you thinking?"

"I told you, already." He rubbed the side of his head and scowled.

She gave him a swift punch in the gut. "You have two minutes to explain yourself." she stomped on his foot.

Wift's green eyes were full of anger and pain, both of which Bera had just inflicted. "Explain what, exactly? I did not do this." He gritted between clenched teeth.

"You killed a nilaon. Do you know how much the people of Tavdren love torture? Imagine what they will do to you." She leaned in close. "Imagine what I could do to you!"

Wift scoffed. "Oh please, I did nothing of the sort. Even if I had killed my father," he sneered, "with the wave of your hand, you would have me spared. Because you are really running things, aren't you Bera? And you and I both know that you need me alive. Don't you?"

He didn't let her respond. "You didn't think that I'd let you control me the way you've been controlling Lawan's boy. Did you?"

"What-" Bera was momentarily stunned.

"That's a ticking time bomb just waiting to go off. Lawan is patient. She'll wait as long as it takes to get what she wants. Just because things have been quiet for a while, doesn't mean that she isn't scheming with him as we speak." Wift took another step back. "You're not the only one who knows how to use their keeper for personal gain. Tavious overheard him talking to Lawan."

She growled and swung another hit. Wift stepped back before the blow could land.

Wift whispered. "Don't believe me? You'll see."

"You're trying to take the blame off yourself. Taking your vengeance on a nilaon was dangerous and foolish."

"You're only angry because your puppet is gone." Wift tilted his head. "Perhaps this makes you vulnerable."

Bera and Wift stared at each other for a long moment. She wasn't sure he was speaking the truth about Moccasin and Lawan. He had the upper hand, and she hated him for it. No one had ever put her in this position. Jin had tried. Atticus thought he could, but no one had ever succeeded.

Turning on her heels she left, slamming the door behind her. Wift looked around at the buckets and cleaning supplies and a tiny smile appeared and slowly grew. Then came the ticking.

Bera growled low in her throat. "Istrumagi!"

"So...did violence make you feel better?" Challen chided her.

"No," she sighed. "It has failed me." Her head fell into her hands.

"The rivalry between Tavious and Lawan is real. Last time it ended with all of us being cursed to earth."

"We need to tell Moccasin. He might be in danger."

Challen scratched his head. *"No. Let's see where this goes."*

.....

Chapter Forty-Five

"**M**aybe Wift has a point." Challen flinched and raced behind her. "Not about murdering Atticus. But about Lawan. Surely it wouldn't hurt to test Moccasin. If he is fully partnering with Lawan…"

"I don't want to think about this anymore," Bera said quietly and calmly. "I'm going to get some sleep. We'll discuss this tomorrow."

Challen knew better than to argue with her. *"That's a good idea. Get some sleep."* The keeper faded.

Ben was't leaving Wift's side in order to keep him from stirring up more trouble. Bera had assigned Ben the task because he had an un-apologetic lack of respect for personal space even when encountering resistance. She believed he was more than capable for the job, and he was honored to be trusted.

Her main concern was for her best friend. Moccasin might now be under the complete in-fluence of Lawan. If this wasn't enough, now he was clearly in danger of Wift. Challen had explained that Tavious' host wasn't the type to know your secret and keep it without some kind of return.

Moccasin can take care of himself, surely.
He's an experience highrindh.

She gently smacked her cheeks. Bera needed this time to rest. There was no time for worry. "It'll be okay." She whispered into the mir-ror. "We'll figure this out."

"You got this!" Challen appeared behind her reflection. *"We'll find a way around Wift."*

.....

"What did he tell you?" Bera calmly asked Ben. They were sitting beside each other on a bench overlooking the fields. Vali was curled up under the bench with her nose between Bera's boots. Her steamy breath billowed out in front of them in the crisp morning air.

Bera held a cup of hot cocoa between her fingers. Ben had sworn the drink would not dis-appoint after bringing a cup one morning. They had been meeting before breakfast for several days to share information on Wift, Moccasin, and all the rumors spinning through the fort.

"He is acting out of anger. I think he is getting help from Tavious. The keeper who-"

"-is sharing his body. Yes, I know."

Through the experience, she'd learned that Ben also knew about his own keeper named Venner. After all these years, it was refreshing to speak openly with someone about the keepers and having help.

He nodded and shut his violet eyes; his hands were steepled in front of him. "Okay. Here's where we are. Moccasin believes the poison was meant for him. He's convinced of it."

"Yeah, he is being stubborn. Can't convince him he wasn't the target."

"Well, if we turn Wift in as the murderer, then Moccasin will think that Wift was the one who tried to kill him. And we both know how that will end."

"Moccasin will go after Wift."

"Bad joo-joo." Ben shook his head. "Very bad."

"But we can't just let Wift get away with it without consequences. He murdered Atticus for gods' sake." She lowered her tone in case anyone was listening. Bera was also not happy with Wift holding cards against her. He'd made it clear that he knew her power was in controlling Atticus. He'd permanently removed that and was now holding it over her. She was searching for some way to regain the upper hand.

Ben opened his eyes wide. "I have an idea. But it's definitely a last case scenario."

"Skates, I'm open to suggestions."

Ben scooted himself closer on the bench. "Wift and I could go to Drundra and find Sundra's host, Chione. That way Wift and Moccasin are kept apart, and they have time to cool off before the last host gets here."

"Hmm." Bera nodded.

"It buys us time."

His plan had merit. She wouldn't lose her friend. And if anything, it would give Moccasin and Wift time to calm down. They might be able to get the keepers to their realm without any more trouble.

"As much as I trust you, I don't trust Wift. And I don't see him suddenly becoming cooperative about going to Drundra. He might resist the very idea. And a long journey with you might just drive him over the edge."

Ben smiled. "I won't take offense to that."

"You should."

It was obvious that Ben had befriended Wift long before the incident. The last thing they needed was to take sides.

Ben stayed positive. "The murder was revenge. I don't think Wift is reckless."

Bera frowned purposely and sipped her cocoa. "That kid has some issues."

"...true..." Ben agreed. "Hey, maybe we

could wipe his memory? Like in the movies!"

"Amusing."

"For real! I saw this sci-fi flick with my cousin, Jerold, at a drive-in, where this man worked for an international mob-"

"Just stop."

.....

Bera needed to ascertain if Moccasin was communicating with his keeper as Challen, and now Wift claimed. In all their years together as friends, she had not once felt that he was under Lawan's control. So, the next morning she rose early and followed Moccasin. Based on experience with her keeper, if he was communicating with Lawan she would be able to tell.

She and Challen had determined that it was best for Challen to stay in hibernation. Removing him would make it difficult for Lawan to sense his presence, especially because he was a young keeper whom she'd not known well.

Moccasin's daily schedule varied little. She found him in the stable tending to the horses. Behind the stables, Bera eased between a stack of lumber that had been propped against the exterior wall and a stall window. Inside, Moccasin was going about his chores. He came and went from her view several times, but nothing unusual occurred.

Bera was considering leaving, when the sound of his voice suddenly reached her outside the barn. And then it was quickly hushed. Something had caught him off guard. She leaned closer to the window opening.

Her fears were confirmed when he began whispering to himself. Any passerby would only see a man talking quietly to himself as he went about his work, but Bera knew better. From what Moccasin was saying, it was obvious to Bera that he'd been communicating with his keeper for some time. Which now made him a very real and dangerous threat.

She now understood the gravity of her situation. Moccasin was convinced someone in the fort was trying to murder him. Uncharacteristically, he was behaving erratically and paranoid. And now, she had confirmation that Lawan was driving this behavior.

Having heard all she needed, Bera began to ease away from the wall when her boot slipped off on rock and knocked over a wooden plank. Cursing herself, she immediately fled into the forest before Moccasin could spot her.

Or so she thought.

.....

Challen shouted as Bera slammed her chamber door. *"Wift was right!"*

"They're communicating. But she's not in complete control. Not fully using his body, anyway."

"Don't be a fool, Bera!"

She muttered and clenched her fists together. "What exactly do you want me to do? Say, hey you know that ghost that's camping out inside of you, are you conspiring with her? Because that would be stupid! He's paranoid enough as it is. That would just turn him against me!"

"It sounds bad when you say it like that!"

"It's bad no matter how it's said, Challen. Give me some room to think." She demanded and watched in relief as the keeper faded back into his hibernation.

"Thank the gods." She practically fell onto her desk, putting her head on her crossed arms. She wanted to scream out her frustration.

Atticus' death had placed an enormous workload onto the three highrindh. Bera in particular, for she was the longest-reigning highrindh and most likely to take the position of nilaon once things calmed.

Bera wasn't sure she would accept the position of nilaon if the other two highrindhs offered. She'd always ruled behind the curtain, and because of that, she was able to move freely among Tavdren. Ruling as nilaon would be suffocating. Constricting her movements and relationships while at the same time adding much more responsibility. Her reputation as highrindh was enough.

At this time, word of Atticus' death would have certainly reached the other regions. They would pounce on this opportunity. This was a precarious situation for Tavdren. The slightest predicament could start a fire of inter-regional turmoil. This is what the highrindh were trying to avoid.

And now Moccasin is communicating with Lawan.

I've spent centuries spinning this web and now it's all coming unraveled.

That afternoon, Moccasin came to her door. He was there to raid her pantry because he felt uncomfortable eating anything from his rooms after the poisoning. She wasn't sure how to behave, so she pretended to work at her desk while he rummaged among her supplies.

Knowing that he was communicating and potentially working with Lawan made her suspicious of his motives for being there. He didn't mention Lawan, and Bera doubted he would ever confide in her. Her mind was buzzing with possible ways to approach the subject as Moccasin sat across from her and munched on an apple. He made idle talk about patrols and problems with schedules.

He is trying to act casual.

What is he up to?

He's looking for something...what?

There was a long, undisturbed silence. It concerned her, this awkward quiet between them. Bera was wracking her brain trying to figure out what he could be looking for.

"Something wrong?"

Moccasin's eyes suddenly stopped moving over her rooms and stared blankly off to the side. He pointed with his half-eaten apple. "Your um...coat."

She glanced over his shoulder to where he was looking. Her armoire was left open. It was her black cloak.

"Yes. That's my cape."

"It's new?" He chewed slowly, eyeing her too closely.

"Yeah." Bera swallowed, trying to figure out where he was leading her. "It is new."

There was a long silent moment between them.

"Don't think I've seen you in it..."

"Probably not. Dunno." Bera almost jumped out of her chair when Vali barked from one of the rooms.

Moccasin scratched his head. "Funny thing is. I have seen you in it. Recently."

"Mm-Hmm."

What is he getting at?

"You were wearing it at the barn earlier this morning. Weren't you, Bera?"

Bera took a deep breath. The memory came back to her. She'd worn the cloak when spying on him at the stables.

The two locked eyes and waited for the other to say something.

.....

Bera looked up from her notes and took a deep breath. "Alright. Let's talk."

"Yeah, that's a good idea, Buddy." The last

word was uttered with a sneer.

"Moc, I had to make sure-"

"Why were you spying on me?" Moccasin was more upset than Bera had ever seen him, including the night of Atticus' murder. His fists were clenched, and his boot tapped the floor with pent-up anger.

"Did you try to poison me?" His eyes were clouded with paranoia. "Was it you?"

"Calm the hell down, Moccasin, and remember who you're talking to."

His eyes bulged, "You're threatening me now!"

She held her hands up. "Please. No. I only needed to see if you were communicating with Lawan."

There was a stunned, silent moment as her words penetrated his anger.

Moccasin exhaled loudly. "How did-" He rubbed his bearded chin, "How do you know about her?"

"About Lawan?" Bera shrugged. This was a conversation, long coming. "I've known since you got here. And I bet you know about me, and the others."

Bera had been dreading this moment for over a hundred years. At this point, she could not lie anymore. He knew about the keepers; she would have to face that. It all had to come out.

Bera told him all she could. About the keepers, her plans, and even her knowledge of

Jin's death and burial. She felt sick in her stomach as the words poured out. Moccasin's pained and outraged expression made her want to turn away, but the lies had to end. So, she faced him.

Bera withheld some things from him, however. Her knowledge of Wift being guilty of Atticus' murder would send Moccasin into a rage that could push Lawan into action. There was no point in telling him. It would only make matters worse.

She also kept secret her years of manipulating Atticus and encouraging Moccasin's drinking to keep him from becoming a greater threat. Bera felt that these details would cloud over the larger issue of how to contain Lawan and whatever she was planning.

Halfway through, Moccasin shot up from his seat and began pacing furiously. Vali sensed the danger and watched him from her place beside Bera. "You knew about Lawan for how long?"

"Er...I wasn't keeping track..."

"Bera!" he snarled.

Vali rose to all fours and laid her ears back, warning him. Bera held her hands up. "The moment I saw you in the Waking Center. Challen told me."

"Why didn't you warn me? You should have said something!"

"It was for your own good." She desperately tried to defend her actions. "We thought that keeping you away from the truth was the best way to keep you away from Lawan. It was clear she was dormant and you knowing about her would only have stirred her."

"We?"

"Challen and I."

When she'd finished and there was nothing more to say, Moccasin quietly walked out of the suite. Bera had absolutely no clue what to do to prevent him from going, so she let him leave and stared as the door closed silently.

Vali sat on her haunches and turned her head to her friend. The wolf was relaxed now that the danger had passed.

This isn't good.

Maybe I shouldn't have told him.

"*You had to,*" Challen muttered from behind her.

.....

Bera stood just to the side of the armory door, listening to Moccasin give warnings to the two soldiers that had been out past curfew.

"Very sorry, Sir. It won't happen again!"

Moccasin's jaw tightened and his nostrils flared. He stared at them and muttered, "If I hear another complaint about you, it will mean kitchen detail for six months."

The soldiers nodded respectfully as they exited the armory office. For the past few days, she'd tried to speak with Moccasin. However, he wouldn't so much as look in her direction. Even

Ben, who'd had a certain ability to charm even the hardest of personalities, couldn't get him a word with him.

Though Moccasin's paranoia had abated, it had been replaced with despondency and disappointment. Bera wasn't sure which was worse.

After the men had retreated down the hall, Bera entered the office and greeted him cautiously. "Moc."

Moccasin rewarded her with his shoulder as he brushed past and out of the room. She was growing very frustrated with his stubborn refusal to discuss the looming threat of Lawan. He either didn't consider her a threat, or he was under her control.

"You're being an idiot! Why won't you listen to reason?" she yelled without thinking.

Moccasin halted just outside the door and slowly turned. He didn't say a word, only glared at her.

"If she needs to, she'll kill you to get her revenge. She doesn't care if you die." Bera clenched her fists together in exasperation.

"I have nothing to say to you." he whispered and left.

Bera stalked to the door and yelled after him, "Oskilgetinn!"

He'll have to talk with me eventually.

.....

"Bera!" Ben called out to her as she took her seat in the dining hall amongst the soldiers.

The high table was no longer a welcoming place to dine with Atticus' recent death and Moccasin's foul mood hanging over like a storm cloud.

Ben pulled up a seat and watched her tear into a roll. "We have a problem."

Bera turned to face him, sighing. "What is it now, Skates?"

His purple eyes darted between them. "You remember how you had me searching Wift's rooms for the poison?"

"Yes."

"Well, it isn't there! And-"

"Spit it out!" Bera tossed her bread on the plate. "What's he done?"

"Okay, Boss." Ben took a deep breath. "Wift planted the half-empty vial of sanguis poison."

"-He did what?"

"Wift planted the vial of sanguis poison in Moccasin's room! Someone, I assume Wift, left a note on Grace's door. She had Moccasin's suite searched, and they found it! He's being arrested, right now."

"You're kidding me, right?" Bera hissed, but she knew he wasn't. Glancing around the hall confirmed that Grace and Moccasin were both absent. "Why would she do this without me?"

"I...I don't know!" Ben shook his head. "Maybe because you and Moccasin are...were friends?"

Bera glared at him and seriously asked, "Are your fingers crossed?"

"I wish." Ben answered, "but no."

Bera pushed away from the table and was running to the exit when a commotion came from further down the main hall. Hurrying to see what was taking place, but knowing already what it was, Bera nearly stumbled in her haste to prevent another disaster.

Her chest went cold as she ran. Bera recalled that Wift had told her he knew Lawan was active. She remembered that Wift's keeper was Tavious, Lawan's natural enemy.

Wift planted the vial to frame Moccasin. *Of course.*

.....

Chapter Forty-Six

Bera was lying on her bed staring at the ceiling. She had a cool towel over her forehead and her feet propped up on a cushion. Vali gnawed on a bone looking up at Bera occasionally with raised eyebrows.

"Well...with Moccasin in a cell, he'll be away from Wift." Challen tried to soothe her.

Earlier, when Bera had caught up to the guards escorting Moccasin to the highrindh office, she saw he wasn't protesting. His eyes were focused on the back of the guard's head directly in front of him. He'd been bound but was cooperating.

She swallowed the stab of guilt that was choking her. Preventing her from calling out to him. It infuriated her that Grace was leading the escort. The other highrindh had taken it upon herself to make the arrest without consulting her peer. The arrest had been made into a public spectacle, with soldiers lining the hall and coming out from various rooms to stamp their boots in approval. The stone walls echoed the thunderous noise.

Bera was helpless to do anything but follow the train of guards. Her eyes fixed on the man walking down the center who towered above the others. His dark head never once turned to the left or right. He was her friend, and she'd do whatever she could to mend this misunderstanding.

Grace took him into the highrindh office, while Bera dispersed the crowd. Once she had the hallway cleared, Bera joined her fellow highrindh. She and Grace sat across Moccasin.

Moccasin's denial sounded weak even to her ears, and she knew the truth. He didn't protest the arrest. He sat in the chair, with his bound hands in his lap, and stared out the window behind them.

I wish he would just look at me!
I want him to be outraged!

Without a nilaon in place, she and Grace would determine Moccasin's punishment. In previous cases, though rare, murder was punished by execution. The Fort's inhabitants had been made to believe that Atticus' death had been accidental. Now they knew their nilaon had been assassinated. Rumors of the anonymous letter about the vial being in Moccasin's room spread quickly, and the residents were demanding justice for their nilaon.

Bera couldn't imagine how to defend Moccasin when he wasn't aggressively claiming his innocence.

On top of everything else, Moccasin was the mage who had, following Atticus' orders, threatened many of the soldiers in the past hundred years. Atticus had used him as a henchman for too long, and the soldiers feared and resented Moccasin. This didn't help his case in the public forum. In the end, it was his word against the false evidence. The letter and the vial.

He is innocent.

But only three of us know it.

And one of us is the murderer.

Wift.

Grace wouldn't hear of taking any action in Moccasin's defense. Though he trained her, Grace wanted to please the residents, even if that might mean betraying her old consultant. It was obvious to Bera that Grace was positioning herself to become nilaon.

Challen nudged her out of her memories. *"What I'm saying is, maybe this was for the best. Now we know that he can't act out and assist*

Lawan. When you're nilaon, you can make sure he's alive yet still contained."

"Mm-Hmm."

"You did everything you were supposed to do. You've taken risks that have paid off. You have real power in this situation. It couldn't have worked out better for us."

"Better for you," Bera mumbled through the towel over her face. "And I told you, I don't want to be nilaon."

If Challen felt any guilt for what happened to Moccasin, he hid it well. *"It's every nephilim for themselves here. You have to accept that."*

"You think I don't know that?" Bera jerked the towel off, "What the hell do you think I've been doing for all these hundreds of years...charity work?"

Maybe I let a friendship get in the way of what's best for me.

Bera felt all the stress, wrecking her physically and mentally. All the strategy and double-dealing. The risks of blackmailing Atticus and keeping several other highrindh in line. It had not been easy. And it was all for ancient keepers who wouldn't even cooperate and didn't even belong here. The quicker she could get rid of the keepers the better.

And then it hit her. When Bera realized what she had to do, a slow smile spread across her face. Bera leaped off the bed and stumbled over Vali. "You're right. It is every nephilim for themselves. I can't let my friend be locked up for something he didn't do." She reached for a sheathe secured to her right thigh. "I'm sorry, Challen. I just can't."

"*Bera...*" Challen tried to block her way, but she walked through him. "*What are you thinking?*"

Her fingers closed around the dagger and checked that it was properly sharpened. "Taking a risk." She held it calmly in her fist. "It's what I do, right? Take risks? Thank you, Challen for reminding me."

Challen rushed to the door. "*Stop!*"

"Your plan is foolish. If we keep him imprisoned, he'll never help us when we need him." She stalked through him and out of the room. "And we will need him for the return spell. So, I say we are doing my plan. Which is, having no plan at all and kicking some ass."

.....

In the southern tower, Bera took the stone stairs descending to the lowest level of the fort. The prison was accessible to highrindh and guards on duty. The most dangerous prisoners were kept here, as all minor infractions were punished with room arrest or additional service detail.

Using her master key, she unlocked the doors to the upper levels of the dungeon and step by step she hurried down to the lower cells. Torches hanging periodically along the walls transformed her passing figure into eerily distorted shadows. The stairwell became narrow, and her footsteps on the uneven stone treads echoed of the thick, stone walls pressing in on her. The echo acted as a signal to the guards below, who would be alerted that someone was descending. This alarm allowed the guards to issue a challenge to any intruder.

No challenge from the guards came forth.

At the receiving area, Bera expected to see an armed guard stationed at the thickly barred gate entrance. But to her confusion, there were no guards in sight.

"Guard?"

"*I don't like this, Bera.*" Challen hissed, irritated that he'd been unable to stop her.

She waved him off and held the dagger close to her chest. The lights were low and the cold air felt electric. Unlocking the iron gate, they stepped cautiously into the depths of the darkened cellblock.

All was silent.

Beside her in the dim light, Challen whispered, "*Where is everyone?*"

"Guard on watch, show yourself!" She commanded.

There was no sound. Along with the lack of guards, the ominous silence drove her heart to hammer her chest.

Carefully, Bera eased around the corner, casting a shield for light and defense. She didn't know what to expect, but what she found frightened her.

The first guard was laying on his back dead from a gash running across his chest. The wound bore evidence of being formed by a cast.

Challen gasped at the sight. Bera instinctively held an arm out to prevent him from passing.

Further in, they discovered four more guards lying dead or stunned. As they crept past the individual prison cells, Bera's cast light revealed that the inhabitants were backed to the farthest ends of their cells with their eyes bulged out and their lips set in a grim line. Their faces were frozen in terror. Their stiff bodies cowered from an unseen menace.

"What's happened to them?" she asked, her eyes resting on a prisoner whose mouth was frozen in a muted scream.

"They've been Chastened," Challen explained. *"Chasten is a keeper spell that restrains its victim, prohibiting movement and sound."*

Bera spotted the magus cell that had once housed the hex, and she quickened her pace. She needed to confirm her dreadful fear. She knew Moccasin would be gone. She knew it without any doubt. And she knew it would mean trouble for them all.

Keeper and host stopped at the open cell. Bera's cast illuminated a blood-red glow on the wall at the back of the cell. It spelled a single word.

Lawan.

"We're too late." Challen groaned.

"What does this mean?" She asked, staring at the blood-written word.

Challen shook his head helplessly. *"Lawan got here first."*

Bera stepped cautiously into the cell. She spotted the source of the blood as a dead guard slumped against the cell wall. She noticed the wound on his neck and quickly looked away.

"He can't have gotten far," Challen murmured next to her. *"Maybe we could catch him?"*

Bera pointed to the blood written word. "There may not be *a him* anymore."

"You don't know for certain."

She shook her head defeated. "Who else could have Chastened the prisoners?" The thought was halted by a slow realization.

For years she'd been dreading this moment when Lawan would take full control and unleash chaos. Yet her reaction wasn't at all how she'd imagined. Bera felt a strange sense of calm as if a weight had been finally lifted from her shoulders. She was a person made for action and had been in a holding position for far too long.

Bera looked back at the cell, assessing her options. She took a deep breath. In the back of her mind, she could smell smoke seeping into the cells.

.....

Bera stood on a hill next to the fort, Vali at her heels. All but the timber roofing in the ancient stone fortress was impervious to the fire. She watched the surrounding forest slowly become consumed by the undefeated flames. The animals had been corralled in the training field, as the soldiers fought to keep the fire from spreading to the outbuildings. An orange moon hung its full head, observing with sorrow the destruction and mayhem. The advancing flames lit up the night sky obscuring the stars with dense, brown smoke. Flames which she knew were lit by Lawan.

Moccasin is gone.

No one else would do this.

No one else would dare.

She could hear someone approach her. Ben's calming voice came from behind. "What do we do now, Boss?"

"We wait for the last host." Her fists clenched tightly digging her nails into the palms of her hands. The approaching fire was drowned out by a burning desire for revenge. "Then we go kill a keeper."

.....

Epilogue

Lawan brought her horse to a steady canter. She had a lot of ground to cover before morning. It had been many centuries since she'd felt the rush of flying through the night on horseback. In the distance, she could smell the smoke from Tavdren's fort.

It would take time to adjust to this new body, but time was the one thing she had. The one thing that hadn't failed her in the past. Patience, yes, that had always been her strength. Others lacked the willingness to wait out their opponents. Not defeating Tavious at the fort was only a minor impediment. Undeterred, she would find a place and settle in to await whatever threats the keepers sent her way. They would come, and she would be prepared. The advantage was hers.

The former host of this body was pushed down far inside where he couldn't interfere. She needed nothing from him now, but his physical form. Douglas had served his purpose.

Now it was her turn.

Lawan had much experience in facing keepers in her home realm. This would be quite simple compared to what she'd wrought in the past. She planned to kill the other keeperial beings once they were gathered together in their hosts. If their hosts died in Hazdrim, the keepers were gone for all eternity. It was a rare chance to permanently end the five keepers who'd destroyed what she most cherished.

The key was in the waiting.

I'll wait as long as I need to.

.....

ABOUT THE AUTHOR

O'merit Kay

O'Merit Kay is a sixteen year old high school student that enjoys reading and writing young adult fantasy fiction. She began writing The Nephilim Realm series two years ago.

She lives in Texas with her family and a three legged dog, Abby May Beans. Her dream is to live on a goat farm and write books.

Made in the USA
Coppell, TX
03 January 2024

27149474R10204